S·O·S at Night

M. A. Wilson

Illustrations by Lizette Duvenage

Rainy Bay Press
Gibsons, BC

Published by Rainy Bay Press
PO Box 1911
Gibsons, BC
V0N 1V0

www.rainybaypress.ca

ISBN: 978-0-9953445-4-9

What people are saying about Maple Harbour Adventures

Adventure on Whalebone Island is a great read, and I cannot wait for the next book in the series. —Teresa Iaizzo, CM Magazine

A great vacation read that every kid should have tucked into their backpack! — Debra Schoenberger, #redhead.with.book

I can wholeheartedly recommend the book to all those seeking a well-crafted adventure story suitable for children ages seven through twelve. — Margaret Lyons, author of Dewi and the Seeds of Doom

Adventure on Whalebone Island may be favourably compared to those (Arthur Ransome) classics, incorporating the key elements on the coast of British Columbia. — Audrey Driscoll, audreydriscoll.com

The book follows classic children's adventure story lines... a fun book for children under 12. — Jan Degrass, Coast Reporter

I loved the book! It had mystery, and I'd love to be on an adventure just like these kids in the story. — Ava, age 10

What a great story! All of the adventures kept me reading and reading! — Bax, age 7

It reminded me of falling in love with reading classic adventure stories as a child. — Maria M., parent

To Kylie

Table of Contents

~1~

Lost in the Fog

Pegasus drifted silently through the water, surrounded by a thick, impenetrable fog. The four children peered into the gloom, but they could hardly see past the bow of the boat. The only sound was the occasional creak of the tiller as Claire turned it first one way and then the other.

"This is weird," whispered Nathan. "I've never been in fog this thick before." There was no need to whisper, but the eerie silence made him reluctant to speak too loudly.

"I don't think I've ever been right in the middle of a fog bank before," said Kendra, also keeping her voice low. "I had no idea it would be so cold!"

"And wet," said Ryan, wiping little drops of moisture off the mast with his hand.

They had only been drifting in the fog for a few minutes. It had been a beautiful sunny day with a light breeze when they set off from Pirate Cove that morning and they had made good time as they sailed out into the strait. But suddenly the wind died and soon after they noticed a large fog bank moving toward them. It enveloped the little boat and its occupants in a cold, damp embrace.

Meg was lying in the bottom of the boat, her head on her paws and her ears flat. She looked very unhappy and not her usual self. Nathan rubbed her head and she looked up at him dolefully.

"We'd better paddle," sighed Claire. "Who knows how long we'll be stuck here otherwise."

Kendra jumped at the chance to do something active. She had been getting quite chilled sitting still in the fog. Picking up the paddle, she reached over the side and dipped it into the water. *Pegasus* began to glide forward, causing wisps of fog to swirl around the bow.

Kendra and Ryan had only just arrived in Maple Harbour late the previous evening. They were back unexpectedly, having already spent part of their holidays with their cousins Claire and Nathan earlier that summer. But while their mom was back east visiting friends, their dad had been called away on a last minute business trip. He had given them a choice—to have an elderly neighbour come and look after them, or stay with Aunt Jennie and Uncle William. It was an easy decision. Ryan and Kendra loved visiting Maple Harbour. They could play on the beach, swim in the ocean, and go sailing in Claire's boat, *Pegasus*. Although they had to cancel a swim camp Kendra had been registered in, she didn't mind. She would much rather swim in the ocean. And whenever they were in Maple Harbour, all sorts of mysteries and adventures seemed to follow them.

"Do we have any idea where we're going?" asked Ryan after a while. "It looks the same in every direction."

"Hmm, good point," said Claire. "We should look at the compass and chart."

Nathan opened a hatch near the front of the boat and rummaged about. He pulled out a laminated plastic chart and a compass and passed them back.

"How will the chart help us if we can't see where we are?" asked Kendra.

"I know roughly where we were when the fog rolled in," said Claire, staring at the chart. "The problem is, we don't know how big this fog bank is or where it goes. And the tide has been carrying us along as well."

"We're heading northeast right now," said Ryan, picking up the compass and holding it out in front of him.

"Really?" said Claire, looking puzzled. "I thought we were going south. We must have paddled around in a circle."

"That doesn't surprise me," said Ryan. "It's pretty disorienting."

"Well, the fog usually stays near the shore. So let's go further out by heading west." Claire turned the tiller. "You guide me with the compass."

Kendra, who had paused to rest while this discussion was going on, began to paddle again. Ryan watched the compass and called out instructions to Claire to adjust her course one way or the other. But rather than coming out of the fog, they seemed to be going deeper into it.

In the distance they could hear the sound of a foghorn, with its deep, lonely voice echoing across the water. "Foggg-eeee. Foggg-eeee."

After a while, Kendra and Nathan switched places. Kendra's arms were tired from paddling. She thought her arms were pretty strong from all the swimming she did, but paddling seemed to be a completely different motion.

Nathan started off paddling enthusiastically and they moved quickly through the water. But soon he began to tire as well and their pace slowed. At one point it looked like the fog was clearing, but then the murky cloud closed around them again.

"How big is this fog bank?" said Nathan exasperatedly, pulling up the paddle and resting for a moment.

Suddenly, there was a deafening blast from a ship's horn immediately in front of them. The sound reverberated all around, causing them to jump in shock. Meg scrambled to her feet, looking around nervously and giving a little bark.

The four children stared out in horror. Looming above them, only a short distance away, was the bow of a huge freighter. And it was coming straight toward them!

~2~

Opera Island

"Paddle!" yelled Claire as she turned the tiller to steer *Pegasus* away from the freighter. Nathan, who had been staring up at the immense ship in shock, began to stroke furiously, sending up splashes of cold water. Ryan and Kendra reached over the other side and desperately tried to paddle with their hands. Claire held her breath as *Pegasus* slowly moved through the water.

Although it seemed like an eternity, it was probably only a few seconds before they were out of the way of the freighter. Ryan, realizing that paddling with his hands was doing little to help, sat up and looked back at the ship.

"Wait a minute," he said, in a voice that was remarkably calm considering the situation. "It's not moving."

Claire and Kendra looked more closely. It was true, the ship wasn't moving. There was no wake at the bow and the water all around was still. Just visible through the fog, a great anchor chain emerged from an opening in the hull and disappeared into the water. Leaning over a railing high above, a small figure in a yellow raincoat looked down at them. He waved. Kendra raised her arm weakly and waved back.

"Okay Nathan, you can stop paddling now," said Claire.

"No way! I'm not stopping until we're out of this fog," he replied, keeping his head bent over the side as he thrust at the water.

The others burst out laughing in relief. Their hearts were still racing from what they had thought was a very close call. Kendra bent down and put her arms around Meg, who gave her face a comforting lick.

They continued to move away from the freighter and soon it was lost to view. Suddenly it began to get brighter and a few moments later they could see pale blue sky poking through the mist above them. Abruptly, they emerged from the fog bank into bright sunshine and blue sky.

"Hooray!" they all cheered as they felt the warm sun on their faces. Everyone was very relieved to get out of the cold, clammy fog and its potential dangers.

"We'd better keep paddling until we're well away from here," said Claire, "or the fog bank might move back over us."

Ryan took over paddling from Nathan and soon they had moved a good distance away. But there was still no wind and it looked like they might be stuck for some time.

"What will we do now?" said Kendra, as Ryan stopped paddling and *Pegasus* slowly drifted to a stop.

"Isn't that the old lighthouse over there?" said Nathan. "Let's go check that out." He pointed to a small rocky island with a tall white tower.

"Oh, wow, we're near the lighthouse!" Claire sounded surprised. "The tide must have carried us a long way north. Well, why don't we visit it, since we're here? As long as you don't mind some more paddling," she added, looking at Ryan. He answered by taking up the paddle again and soon they were making their way toward the island.

As they got closer, the island and its lighthouse began to take shape. The island itself was little more than a pile of rocks, perhaps fifty metres across at its widest point. There were no trees, only a few scraggly bushes. A couple of seals lolled near the water's edge, their heads turning toward the little boat and its occupants as they approached. A number of gulls and other seabirds were perched on the rocks at one end of the island.

"Isn't that the old lighthouse over there?"

The lighthouse was situated at the highest point, which was only a few metres above sea level. It was a tall white tower in the shape of a hexagon, which tapered slightly as it rose so that the top was narrower than the bottom. Near the top was a small balcony that ran all the way around. Above that was the light room, with glass windows facing in every direction. The balcony and light room were painted red, but the paint was faded and several of the windows appeared to be broken. Attached to the base of the tower was a small rectangular building, also painted white.

"I've never been to a lighthouse before," said Kendra. "What's the name of it?"

"It's the Opera Island Lighthouse," said Nathan. "And this is Opera Island."

"Why is it called Opera Island?" said Ryan.

Nathan shrugged. "I don't know." He looked at Claire, who shook her head as well.

"Maybe the seals sound like opera singers when they bark," said Kendra with a smile. As if it heard her, one of the seals let out a series of mournful barks before sliding into the water.

Perched on another rock a short distance away was a smaller, more modern looking light. It was built on a black metal frame with a solar panel attached to the side to it.

"What's that?" asked Ryan, pointing at the smaller light.

"They closed the old lighthouse years ago and replaced it with that new automatic one," said Claire. "A lighthouse keeper used to live here in the old days though."

"That would be so cool!" said Kendra. "I'd like to be a lighthouse keeper and live on an island."

"You can if you want," said Nathan. "Some of the lighthouses still have keepers who live in them. Just not this one."

"I don't know. It could be pretty lonely out here," said Ryan skeptically. He thought he would get bored quickly with only seagulls and seals for company.

By now they had reached the island. Claire steered them toward a spot where the rocks were low and it looked like they could land. There were old pilings in the water and bits of concrete and twisted metal on the rocks. Holding the bow rope, Nathan hopped onto the rocks, followed closely by Meg. He tied the rope to a metal post that was set into the rock.

"Was this an old dock at one time?" asked Kendra.

"I think so," said Claire. "This is the most sheltered spot on the island. Although none of it is very protected," she added. "I don't think they could have kept a boat here permanently. It was probably just used to land supplies."

Once *Pegasus* was secured, the rest of them jumped out and began to explore the island. Near the lighthouse, they found some old concrete foundations.

"This must have been the light keeper's house," said Ryan. "That little building attached to the lighthouse is too small to live in."

"Yes, I think the old house got vandalized and they tore it down," agreed Claire.

Together they peered up at the smooth walls of the lighthouse tower. On one side there was a heavy wooden door with a large lock on it. Up close, they could see the white paint was peeling and faded, exposing the concrete in places.

They walked around to the other side where the attached building stuck out. It had a small steel door with a combination lock, the kind with a series of numbered dials on the side. There were no windows or other openings.

"It must be pretty dark in there," said Kendra.

As they walked around the attached building, they noticed a large sign on a post driven into the rocks. It was facing out to sea, so they wandered over to read it. They were surprised to see it was a realty sign that read FOR SALE, with a name and telephone number below.

"How can a lighthouse be for sale?" said Ryan. "Isn't it owned by the government?"

"Maybe we can buy it!" said Nathan. "I'm not sure I want to be a lighthouse keeper, but it sure would be cool to own an island and an abandoned lighthouse! Just imagine!"

"I guess the government can sell it if they want to," said Claire thoughtfully. "But I've never heard of one being for sale around here before."

The four continued their exploration of the island, with Kendra and Nathan chattering about what they would do with the island if they bought it.

"I would turn the light room into a bedroom," said Nathan.

"Yes," said Kendra. "And make the roof all glass so we could look at the stars at night!"

There wasn't much else to see on the island, so they made their way back to *Pegasus*. A light breeze had picked up and the previously glassy water was now rippled with small waves.

"We should get going before the wind dies down again." Claire looked around for Meg, who was sniffing at the old house foundations. "Meg!" she called, but the dog ignored her. They walked over to see what she was doing.

"What are you sniffing at?" said Kendra as they came closer. Meg had her nose in a space between the concrete and the rocks. She pawed at the space and whimpered softly.

"Don't do that Meg. You'll get your paw stuck." Nathan pulled her away and, getting down on his hands and knees, put his arm into the space and felt around. He pulled out a clump of seaweed and dropped it on the rock beside him. In the middle of the seaweed was a very old and very dirty rubber ball.

Giving a small bark of joy, Meg rushed over and picked up the ball in her mouth. She dashed around excitedly before bringing the ball to Claire and dropping it expectantly at her feet. Claire picked it up reluctantly.

"Ugh, that's disgusting Meg," said Claire, wrinkling up her nose. She threw the ball away and Meg took off after it.

Meanwhile, Nathan was looking closely at the pile of seaweed. He reached in and pulled something out.

"What's this?" He held it up for the others to see.

They crowded around to take a closer look. The object looked like a large steel nail with a wooden handle across the top, making a T-shape. The wood was very old and worn and the metal part was covered in rust. It was a bit larger than Nathan's hand.

"What is it?" asked Ryan. Nathan just shook his head in response.

"It looks like a tool for poking holes in something," said Kendra.

"Except the end of the spike is flat," pointed out Nathan.

"Maybe Mom or Dad will know what it is," said Claire. "Come on, we should go."

They returned to the boat and the others got in while Claire untied *Pegasus* from the post. Meg came racing up and jumped in after them. She had retrieved her ball and lay down with it between her paws.

"You're not bringing that with you!" Nathan took the ball from her and made to throw it back on shore. Meg immediately jumped up, ready to chase after it. Nathan paused.

"Someone hold on to her," he said, "or we'll never get off this island!"

Kendra held Meg's collar and Nathan threw the ball far up toward the lighthouse. As he did so, Claire pushed *Pegasus* out and stepped on board. Meg watched dejectedly as her ball bounced a few times and then disappeared from sight.

"Don't worry, Meg. We'll find you a nice ball when we get back home," said Kendra, patting the dog on the head. But Meg continued to gaze forlornly toward the island as they sailed away.

~3~

"They Can't Do That!"

The wind picked up as they sailed back home, allowing them to cover the distance quickly. The fog bank that had trapped them earlier had disappeared completely, and they could see clear up the coast. It was a gorgeous late summer day with hardly a cloud in the blue sky. They were headed for Pirate Cove, the little bay where Claire and Nathan lived. Its real name was Rainy Bay, but they all agreed that Pirate Cove was a much better name. After all, thought Kendra as she gazed over the bow of the boat, it never seemed to rain when she was there. Then she remembered the huge storm when they had visited earlier that summer. Rainy Bay was certainly a better name for the bay that night!

"Does someone else want to steer?" asked Claire.

"I will!" said Kendra.

Ryan, who had already risen from his seat to take over from Claire, sat back down. He stared at his younger sister as she clambered over the seats to the back of the boat and took the tiller from Claire. Ryan had loved sailing ever since Claire had taught the two of them in *Pegasus* the previous summer. He hated most sports, but sailing was unlike any other sport he had tried. This summer he'd convinced his parents to register him for a sailing course at a yacht club in the city where they lived. The course took place on a lake and the little dinghies they used looked more like bathtubs than sailboats, but it had given him a better understanding of how to sail. Now he was eager to put what he learned into practice, so he was a bit miffed when Kendra jumped ahead of him. She didn't seem to care about sailing at all and couldn't keep the boat straight to save her life!

Oblivious to Ryan's look, Kendra sat down and took over from Claire. Ryan was wrong to think she didn't care about sailing. Indeed, she enjoyed sailing very much. She just didn't think it was that important to keep a straight course. Unlike Ryan, Kendra excelled at every sport and didn't worry about things too much. If she was doing something wrong, she'd figure it out soon enough. With sailing, it was easy to get confused with so many distractions around her. But she loved the feel of the wind in her hair and the sound of the waves lapping gently on the side of the boat, and she assumed that her skills would improve quickly. So she held on to the tiller happily and guided them on a wobbly course toward home.

They hadn't gone far when Nathan called out from the bow. "There's a log ahead!" he warned.

Kendra looked over Nathan's head and could just make out a dark shape bobbing in the water. She hurriedly turned the tiller. Unfortunately, this was one of those times where she got confused and, in her haste, she pushed the tiller the wrong way. The boat lurched sharply as they turned through the wind, and everybody ducked as the boom swung over their heads.

"Kendra!" said Ryan exasperatedly. "Let me steer!" He took the tiller roughly and pushed her out of the way.

"Give us a warning, Kendra, if you're going to do that!" said Claire with a laugh.

Kendra felt her ears burn. She turned bright red with embarrassment and moved quietly to where Ryan had been sitting. She felt humiliated and resentful toward Ryan for taking over. But mostly angry at herself for making such a careless mistake.

Ryan set them back on course. The lessons had served him well and he soon had *Pegasus* speeding through the water. Claire looked at him approvingly.

Pirate Cove lay between two steep, rocky headlands which guarded its entrance. Arbutus trees, with twisting branches and strange, peeling, reddish-brown bark, clung to the rocks. In the centre of the bay, a small sandy beach sloped gently down to the water, with a dock and a small boathouse at the water's edge. Above the beach, a rickety set of steps led up the bank to the house above.

As they came around the first headland and turned into the bay, they heard the high pitched whine of a boat motor coming from the other direction. Soon a small inflatable dinghy came into sight, moving at high speed and bouncing on the waves. Sighting the sailboat, it turned sharply and came directly toward them without slowing its pace. Claire pursed her lips and frowned but made no attempt to change her course.

"Who's that?" asked Kendra. But as soon as the words were out of her mouth she knew the answer. There were two blond-haired boys in the dinghy, dressed in identical swim shorts and t-shirts. It was the Mitchell brothers, twin brothers who lived nearby. They were Claire's nemesis, always playing pranks and getting themselves into trouble in one way or another.

The dinghy roared up to them and, at the last moment, turned slightly and cut across *Pegasus'* bow. The little sailboat tipped sharply as it was hit by the inflatable's wake.

"Like our new boat?" one of the boys whooped as they went by.

"Get out of here!" shouted Claire angrily. "You know that's dangerous!"

The two boys just hooted with laughter as they turned their boat around and came back to do a full circle around *Pegasus* before zooming off in the other direction.

The children and Meg were tossed from one side to the other as the boat rocked back and forth between the waves. Meg tried to stand up in the bottom, but her feet kept sliding out from under her as the boat swayed.

"I hope they hit a rock," muttered Claire as the dinghy disappeared out of sight.

"I see they haven't changed," said Ryan with a laugh.

Claire shook her head. "Nope." Then she laughed too. "I'd die of shock if they ever did."

They sailed into the bay and pulled up at the dock. Together they hauled *Pegasus* out of the water and took down the sails. They stowed them along with the other gear in the little boathouse before making their way up to the house.

Aunt Jennie and Uncle William were in the kitchen. Aunt Jennie was mixing something in a large bowl while Uncle William was washing dishes.

"You four are late getting back," said Uncle William, looking up from the sink. "You must be hungry."

"Starving!" said Nathan, peering into the bowl. "What's that?"

"Blueberry muffins," Aunt Jennie replied. "But they won't be ready for a while. There's soup on the stove and some bread on the counter."

The four children helped themselves to large bowls of tomato soup and thick slices of bread. The bread was still warm from the oven, and they slathered it with butter before dunking it into the thick, steaming soup. Aunt Jennie was a fabulous cook, and Kendra and Ryan looked forward to every meal during their visits. The soup was rich and delicious, made with fresh tomatoes from the garden. Ryan savoured a mouthful before swallowing it and thought it was the best tomato soup he'd ever tasted. He recalled his mother attempting to make her own tomato soup last winter, which had been a complete disaster. It was back to cans after that.

While they ate, they told Aunt Jennie and Uncle William about their morning adventures; first being lost in the fog and surprised by the freighter, and then landing on Opera Island with the lighthouse. Aunt Jennie and Uncle William looked concerned when they heard about their encounter with the freighter, but then laughed in relief that it had been anchored.

"The fog was certainly thick this morning," said Uncle William. "It came all the way up to the house."

"Do you know why it's called Opera Island?" asked Ryan.

Uncle William shook his head. "I don't know. Maybe one of the light keepers was an opera fan?"

"How's the old lighthouse?" said Aunt Jennie. "I don't think they've been maintaining it."

"The paint looks pretty old and there are some broken windows," said Claire. "But we couldn't see inside, of course."

"We found this though," said Nathan, remembering the strange object he'd found. He reached into his pocket and pulled it out. His mother and father peered at it.

"Do you know what it is?" asked Ryan.

"No," said Uncle William, shaking his head. He held the object up to the light and examined it closely. "It looks like some kind of tool, but I don't know what it would be used for."

"It looks quite old," said Aunt Jennie. "You should take it down to the museum and see if they know what it is."

"That's a good idea," said Claire. "We can go after lunch."

Aunt Jennie handed it back to Nathan, who put it in his pocket.

"Oh, I almost forget to tell you," said Claire, suddenly remembering. "The island is for sale."

"What island?" said Uncle William.

"Opera Island. The one with the lighthouse."

"What!" they both exclaimed at once.

"There's a big FOR SALE sign on it," said Nathan.

"They can't sell Opera Island!" said Aunt Jennie.

"Why not?" said Claire. "That lighthouse hasn't been used for years."

"Opera Island is more than just a few rocks with a lighthouse!" said Aunt Jennie indignantly. "It's one of the most important bird nesting sites on the entire coast!"

~4~

A Visit to the Museum

Claire turned to her mother in surprise. "We saw a few birds there but not that many," she said.

"At this time of year most of them have left," replied Aunt Jennie. "But earlier in the summer you can see hundreds of seabirds nesting there."

"I've never heard of the government selling a lighthouse," said Uncle William, sounding puzzled. "But I suppose it happens sometimes."

"Well, it's not going to happen this time!" declared Aunt Jennie. "I'm going to find out what's going on!" She rose from the table abruptly and stormed out the front door, pausing only to grab her purse and keys on the way out. The others looked at each other in amazement as they heard the car start and then drive away.

"If anyone can stop the sale of that island, it's Mom," said Nathan, turning his attention back to his soup. Uncle William nodded in agreement. When Claire and Nathan's mother put her mind to something, it usually got done. For many years she had helped organize many of the community's volunteer events, and now she was a councillor on the village council.

They finished their lunch and, after helping to clean up, prepared to go to the museum. The previous summer Uncle William had fixed up some old bikes for Ryan and Kendra to use, and now they pulled them out of the shed and dusted them off. The tires were a bit soft, but they found an old pump to inflate them. Once they were done, they hopped on the bikes and joined Claire and Nathan, who were waiting for them in the driveway.

Meg stood by the gate and whined as they prepared to set off. She hated being left behind, but she couldn't keep up when they went off on their bicycles.

"Poor Meg." Kendra gave the dog an apologetic look. "I wish she could come with us."

"Maybe she could," said Ryan. "I saw an old wagon in the shed when we pulled the bikes out. Perhaps we could tow it like a trailer."

"That's a great idea!" said Nathan. He didn't like leaving Meg behind either.

He and Ryan ran to the shed and pulled out the old wagon. It had been given to him for Christmas when he was little and he hadn't used it for years.

The red paint was peeling and the sides were dented, but the wheels still turned.

"I don't know." Claire looked dubiously from the wagon to Meg and back.

"Come on, Meg," said Nathan, patting the bottom of the wagon. Meg wandered over and sniffed inside the wagon, but made no attempt to get in.

Together, Nathan and Ryan lifted her up and placed her in the wagon. Meg looked around for a moment, then promptly hopped back out.

"I know, I'll get some cookies." Nathan ran into the house and came back with a handful of dog biscuits. He showed one to Meg and then tapped the bottom of the wagon. This time Meg didn't hesitate. She jumped in and sat down, looking expectant. Nathan gave her a cookie. "Good dog."

While Nathan fed Meg a steady supply of dog biscuits, Ryan brought his bike over and tied the wagon handle to the rack on the back. He mounted the bike and slowly began to pedal. Meg looked around in surprise as the wagon started to move, but she stayed in.

The others followed as Ryan slowly towed Meg down the driveway. He pedalled a little faster. The wagon began to rattle and shake on the rough dirt driveway. Meg shifted uncomfortably, but she stayed in.

Suddenly the wagon's front wheel hit a deep rut in the road. The wagon lurched to the side, pulling Ryan with it. His bike toppled over and he landed with a thud on the side of the road. Meg, who had jumped out as soon as the wagon started to tip, trotted over and licked his face as he lay there.

"Hmm, maybe this wasn't such a good idea," he muttered as he rubbed his knee. The others, once they knew he wasn't seriously hurt, laughed.

"It looks like you'll just have to stay behind, Meg," said Kendra. But Meg had already wandered off into the trees, following a scent. She had decided that it was best if the children did their biking without her.

They left Meg and continued on their way. It was a short and pleasant ride from the house into Maple Harbour. They followed a trail that led through a forest of tall fir trees. The air was cool and refreshing, and sunlight poked through the trees as they pedalled along. It wasn't too long before they emerged from the forest and joined the road for the last few kilometres into the village.

The museum was located just outside the village centre. Although the museum had been around a long time, it looked new and modern due to a recent expansion and upgrade. They placed their bikes in a new steel rack by the front door and went in.

The museum was dark inside compared to the bright sunshine outside and it took a few moments for their eyes to adjust. A few visitors were looking around. The main hall where they had entered was full of old artifacts from the early settlers on the coast. There were large displays of old logging and fishing gear, and nets and floats hung from the walls. Off to the side in another room was the Grizzly Mask, which the four had helped recover after it was stolen earlier that summer.

In the middle of the main hall was a beautiful hand-made wooden boat. "That's new," said Claire, walking over to it. The others followed her. The boat was quite narrow, like a canoe, but not as long and with oars and a keel. A sign in front of the boat read *Replica – 1930's Handliner.*

"That must have taken a long time to make," said Nathan, running his hand along the beautiful polished wood sides.

"It certainly did," said a voice behind them. They turned to look and saw a young woman standing behind them. Her short, spiky hair was coloured bright pink and she wore a large ring in her nose.

"Two of our volunteers spent nearly a year making it for us," the woman continued. "But I don't think they minded. It was a labour of love. It's an exact copy of a handliner, which was a common type of fishing boat used here 50 to 100 years ago.

"You two must be Ryan and Kendra." She held out her hand to them each in turn. "I'm Sophie."

"Sophie's the new curator for the museum," explained Claire.

Wow, thought Kendra. Sophie didn't look at all what she expected a museum curator to look like.

"Are you just here to look around?" asked Sophie.

"Actually, we have a question for you," said Nathan, pulling the object he'd found out of his pocket. He had wrapped it in an old cloth, which he now removed.

Sophie took the object from him and looked at it closely, turning it over in her hands.

"It looks like a stitch heaver," she said after a few moments. "Where did you find it?"

They told her. "What's it for?" asked Ryan.

"It was used by a sailmaker. They would wrap thread around it so they could pull it tight when they were making stitches. And the end was used to help push needles through the sail."

"How old is it?" asked Nathan, as she handed the stitch heaver back to him.

"It's hard to know for sure, but it was probably made in the late 1800's, during the last days of commercial sailing ships."

"How did it end up on Opera Island?" wondered Kendra.

Sophie shrugged. "One of the light keepers might have owned it, I suppose." She thought for a moment. "Or it could have come from a wreck."

"Cool! Were there wrecks on that island?" asked Nathan. He looked at the stitch heaver with renewed interest.

"I thought the point of a lighthouse was to prevent wrecks," said Ryan.

Sophie laughed. "It doesn't seem to have prevented all of them. There have been a few wrecks in the vicinity over the years. Mostly small boats, but there was one big wreck around the turn of the century. It made headlines across the country.

"We have some information about that wreck if you're interested." She led the way to a large cabinet filled with drawers. Pulling one open, she thumbed through a stack of files and pulled one out, placing it on top of the cabinet.

"Here you go," she said, opening the file folder. Inside were photocopies of old newspaper clippings.

The children gathered around and began to look through the clippings, while Sophie returned to her work. Claire picked up an article dated September 12, 1899, and began to read.

Ship Sinks off BC Coast

The ship _Alexandria_ went down overnight off the coast of BC. The 1500 tonne barque was returning from Skagway to Seattle when it is believed to have struck rocks about two miles offshore. There were reportedly 85 passengers and 17 crew on board. At this time it is not known how many lives may have been lost. A number of passengers were able to swim to safety, while a nearby lighthouse keeper, Henry Cooper, rescued many more. Boats continue to search the area for survivors. The _Alexandria_ is owned by GoldStar Shipping of Seattle and is believed to have been bringing miners back from the Klondike gold fields, many of them penniless.

"Here's another," said Ryan. "This one's from November that same year."

Shipping Line Sued for Negligence

GoldStar Shipping is being sued by survivors and relatives of the deceased from the sinking of the *Alexandria*. The barque went down off the BC coast in September. Eight passengers are known to have drowned and two others are still missing and presumed drowned. The plaintiffs are claiming negligence on the part of GoldStar and the captain and crew of the *Alexandria*, and are demanding compensation for lives and cargo lost. While most of the passengers are thought to have been failed miners returning penniless from the Klondike gold fields, some are claiming that in fact, they were returning with fortunes in gold, which have now been lost. GoldStar, in its defence, has claimed the light on a nearby lighthouse was not lit that night and therefore they could not be held liable for the sinking. None of the claims has yet been heard in court.

"Wow, there could be a fortune in gold at the bottom of the sea!" said Kendra.

"Not likely," said Ryan. "The gold rush was over by 1899 and most of the miners were broke. Only the first few prospectors and the people who sold them supplies made any real money."

They carefully returned the clippings to the file and placed it back in the cabinet drawer. Before they left they looked into Sophie's office to thank her.

"Not a problem," she said. "I'm glad you're interested."

"Do you really think the stitch heaver came from the *Alexandria*?" asked Nathan.

"It's possible," she said. "It was a sailing ship so they would have had those on board. But it could easily have come from somewhere else too."

Nathan reached into his pocket and took out the stitch heaver again. He held it out to Sophie. "Would you like this for the collection?" he asked.

Sophie's eyes lit up. "I'd love it," she exclaimed. "We don't have anything like it."

"It's better if everyone can see it," said Nathan, feeling pleased with himself. He knew Claire was impressed with his act of generosity. "And I can come here to see it anytime I want anyway."

"Thank you very much," said Sophie, taking the tool from him.

"How do you know so much about this stuff?" said Kendra. "You've only been here a few months."

"That's my job!" she said with a laugh. "Actually, I'm still learning a lot about the history of the coast. But some divers were in a little while ago looking for information about shipwrecks to see if there were any potential dive sites."

"That was lucky," said Ryan. "By the way, do you know why it's called Opera Island?"

"Sorry," she said apologetically. "Perhaps old sailors thought the wind blowing around there sounded like an opera. But I really don't know."

~5~

Making Plans

The children said goodbye to Sophie and exited the museum through the front doors. Their bikes were waiting for them where they'd left them in the bike rack. The seats were hot to the touch after sitting in the sun.

"Hmm," said Nathan. "Since we're in Maple Harbour …"

"We should go get ice cream," said Ryan, finishing his sentence for him.

"Exactly! How did you know?"

"It's not too hard to know what's on your mind, Nathan," laughed Ryan. "It's almost always food!"

They turned left out of the parking lot onto the road that led to the village. It only took a few minutes to reach the ice cream shop. There were a number of people eating ice cream outside, and there was a long lineup inside.

They joined the back of the line and waited their turn. Shortly after, the door opened and a police officer walked in and stepped behind them in the lineup.

"Hi Officer Sandhu," said Claire. Maple Harbour's only police officer was a good friend of Aunt Jennie and Uncle William. The four children had got to know him well through the various adventures they'd been mixed up in over the past couple of years.

"Hi kids," he said. "This is a popular place today! I hope this line doesn't take too long."

"Don't worry. We'll save your place in line if any urgent crimes need to be solved," Claire said with a sly smile. He laughed good-naturedly. Maple Harbour was usually a pretty sleepy place when it came to crime.

They chatted with the officer while they waited their turn to order. Officer Sandhu was surprised to see Ryan and Kendra back again so soon and they explained the circumstances that had led to them being in Maple Harbour for a second time that summer. In turn, he filled them in on various goings-on in the village that summer.

"I just saw your mom leaving the realty office," he remarked, looking at Claire and Nathan. "You're not thinking of moving, are you?"

"No, we'd never leave Pirate Cove," said Nathan. He explained about Opera Island and how Aunt Jennie was trying to find out more about the sale.

"That's strange," Officer Sandu said, looking thoughtful. Claire was about to ask him if he knew any more, but they had reached the front of the line and it was their turn to order.

After paying for their cones they stepped outside. All the seats were taken so they found a place where they could lean against the railing.

"Mmm," said Kendra. "My favourite ice cream in the whole world." She had chosen blackberry, and it tasted just like blackberries picked straight from the bush.

They had to eat quickly, as the sun was already causing the cones to melt. Officer Sandhu came out shortly, giving them a quick wave before climbing into his police cruiser and driving away.

Once they had finished, they licked the ice cream from their lips and set off for home on their bikes. By the time they reached the house the sun was beginning to drop and it was getting close to dinner time. Inside, Uncle William was chopping vegetables for a salad while Aunt Jennie was putting some bread in the oven to warm.

"You're just in time," she said as they came in. "Wash up and you can set the table. We're eating in a few minutes." She eyed Nathan, her eyebrows raised.

"Is that ice cream on your face?" she said. He didn't reply but hurried to the bathroom to wash up.

Dinner was a large lasagna, accompanied by Aunt Jennie's home baked garlic bread and a salad from the garden. Ryan didn't think he'd be hungry after a late lunch and the ice cream, but soon he found himself tucking into seconds.

"Did you find out anything more about Opera Island?" Claire asked her mother when they had finished eating. She mentioned that Officer Sandhu had seen Aunt Jennie leaving the real estate office.

"Oh yes, I found out quite a bit," replied Aunt Jennie. "But it's not very good news, I'm afraid.

"The government has indeed put the island up for sale. I spoke with Pete Saunders at the realty office, and he is very surprised by it. He's never seen a government lighthouse up for sale before. He's also surprised at the price, which he thinks is much higher than it's worth." She mentioned the value and Uncle William gave a low whistle.

"Maybe no one will buy it if it's that much," said Kendra.

"That's the bad news," said Aunt Jennie. "Someone has already made an offer."

"What!" they all cried together. "Who?"

"Nobody knows. It's a numbered company. And Pete says they never even came to see him or asked to visit the island. The offer was submitted via a lawyer in the city."

"So is that it?" said Claire. "Does that mean the island is sold?"

"Not quite," said her mother, with a gleam in her eye. "I also spoke with the local government agent. He told me that the government rules for selling property state that the village council has first rights to purchase the land if we can match the asking price. So if we can raise the funds by the closing date, then we can buy it instead of that numbered company."

"When's the closing date?" asked Uncle William.

"That's more bad news. The sale closes at midnight this Saturday."

"Saturday! That's only a few days away," said Claire with dismay.

"We can do it!" cried Kendra. "We could hold a car wash!"

"Or a bake sale!" said Nathan, eyeing up the muffins in a jar on the counter.

"Well, I'm glad you feel that way," said Aunt Jennie. "Because I think we should try. It's not going to be easy, but if the whole community pulls together, I believe we can do it!"

* * *

The house that evening was a hive of activity. Aunt Jennie immediately got on the phone and began calling friends and acquaintances, trying to drum up support for the fundraising effort. The others decided to make posters to place around the village. Nathan pulled a big box of art supplies out from a drawer and placed it on the table. It was filled with different coloured paper, markers, glue, scissors, and paints and brushes.

"But what should I put on the poster?" asked Kendra, picking up a paintbrush. "We don't know what Aunt Jennie is planning for a fundraiser yet."

"We can start with 'Save Opera Island'," said Claire. "Leave some space for details at the bottom and we can add them later."

"I'm going to start by drawing an island," said Nathan.

"And maybe an opera singer," added Kendra. "If I can figure out how to draw one."

They set down to work on their posters. Everyone was soon quiet as they concentrated on their creations. In the background, Aunt Jennie continued to make calls on the phone. After a while, Claire glanced up and looked at the posters taking form around the table.

"You can't put palm trees on the island!" she exclaimed, pointing at Nathan's poster.

"Why not?" he said. "I like palm trees."

"But they don't grow here!"

"Sure they do. There's some on the Parker's lawn. And in front of the hotel in the village."

"Well, they don't grow on Opera Island!" said Claire grumpily.

"There aren't *any* trees on Opera Island," pointed out Ryan. His drawing was a more realistic representation of the island, mostly rocks and a few scrubby bushes.

At that moment Aunt Jennie rejoined them, having finished her calls. They all looked at her expectantly.

"The mayor and the rest of the village council are behind it one hundred percent," she said. "As well as a number of other key people in the community whose support we need. We'll start canvassing for money starting tomorrow. And on Saturday we're going to hold a big fundraising barbecue in the village!

"Which you are in charge of organizing," she added, looking at Uncle William. Uncle William raised his eyebrows questioningly but then nodded his head in assent.

"I better add that information to my poster," said Ryan. Aunt Jennie looked at their posters and nodded approvingly.

"You can finish off your posters, but don't be too long," she said. "It's getting late and we've got a big day tomorrow."

Everyone completed their posters, adding information about the barbecue and how to make donations. Then they got ready for bed.

Lying in bed, Kendra found it hard to fall asleep. It had been a busy day and her mind was spinning. There was always so much going on when they visited Maple Harbour, she thought. Slowly her mind drifted to that morning, when she had turned *Pegasus* the wrong way. The thought of it still caused her to cringe with embarrassment. Not just for making the mistake, but at how Ryan had taken over from her. She didn't blame Ryan for getting upset, although she was a bit surprised—he wasn't usually like that. Instead, she blamed herself for not paying enough attention. Kendra wasn't used to making mistakes or struggling to learn something. Everything always seemed to come easily. But somehow the concepts of sailing seemed to escape her. That needs to change, she thought with determination. I need to learn more about sailing, so there won't be any more incidents like the one today!

~6~

Treasure?

The next morning everyone was up early as there was plenty to do. Now it was Uncle William's turn to be on the phone, making arrangements for the barbecue to be held in a few days. Aunt Jennie was making a long list of people she wanted to call on, looking for donations.

"No pancakes today, I'm afraid," she said to Ryan as he walked into the kitchen. "I've got too much to do." Seeing the disappointment on Ryan's face, she added, "Unless you want to make them."

"Sure!" said Ryan. He had come to expect big healthy breakfasts while staying at his uncle and aunt's. Aunt Jennie was always up early making something in the kitchen. It was a change from home, where breakfast was usually a bowl of cereal eaten in a hurry.

"There's a good recipe for pancakes in that book over there," Aunt Jennie said. "There's blueberries in the fridge and bananas on the counter. Nathan can show you where everything else is."

Ryan opened the book Aunt Jennie had pointed to and found the pancake recipe. Nathan helped and soon the two of them were cooking up pancakes on the griddle.

"Not as good as Aunt Jennie's," said Kendra, taking a bite of the first one. "But not bad."

"Mmm, are those pancakes?" said Uncle William, getting off the phone and coming into the kitchen. He sniffed the air. "Banana?"

"Banana and blueberry," said Ryan, putting a pancake down on a plate in front of him.

Uncle William sat down and began to eat. "The barbecue is coming together," he said between bites. "The grocery store has agreed to provide all the food for free and I've lined up some musicians to perform. And a whole bunch of local businesses have donated raffle prizes. I'll need the four of you to sell raffle tickets on Saturday.

"Best of all," he said with a twinkle in his eye, "we're going to have a dunk tank! And all the village council have volunteered to be dunked to raise money."

"What!" said Aunt Jennie. "I didn't volunteer for that!"

"Not exactly. But the mayor volunteered on your behalf."

"Where are you getting a dunk tank from?" asked Nathan.

"I'm going to build it. One of our neighbours down the road has an old water storage tank they aren't using, and he said we could use that. I'll just build a hinged platform to go over it."

"And you think you can get that done before the barbecue? With everything else to do?" said Aunt Jennie dubiously.

"Piece of cake," said Uncle William, helping himself to another pancake.

"What do you need us to do today, Mom?" asked Claire.

Aunt Jennie looked at the long list of tasks in front of her.

"The print shop is printing up some flyers right now. I'd like you four to pick those up and take them around the neighbourhood. Knock on people's doors and tell them what's going on. We need everyone in Maple Harbour to be aware of our fundraising effort and what a short timeline we have."

"We can put our posters up in the village when we pick up the flyers!" said Kendra.

"That's a good idea," said Aunt Jennie.

They hurriedly finished their pancakes and washed up the breakfast dishes before setting out on their bikes to Maple Harbour. The print shop was on the edge of town, not far from the museum. It was housed in a drab grey warehouse. Leaning their bikes against the side of the building, they pushed open the door and walked in. Stacks of printed paper were piled everywhere, and there was a whir of machinery. In the middle of the room a man sat at a desk, which itself was overflowing with paper. He had a pair of glasses pushed up on his forehead and was peering at a computer screen.

"What do you need?" he said shortly, without looking up.

"We're here to pick up the flyers for the Opera Island fundraiser," said Claire.

"Oh, right." He looked around the room for a moment. "Over there," he said, pointing to a stack of papers on a chair.

Claire picked up the flyers and put them into her backpack.

"That's only half of them," the man said. "The rest will be done in a couple of hours. You'll have to come back." He went back to staring at his computer screen.

Claire thanked him and they left the building.

"He's not very friendly," said Ryan once the door had closed behind them.

"Oh, he's always like that," said Claire. "He seems grumpy, but he's not really so bad. And mom says he's printing these flyers for free to help with the fundraiser."

They hopped back on their bikes and rode on into the village. It was still early and there were few people about. They put up their posters in the locations where they thought they would be seen by the most people. Nathan put his up at the library. Kendra put hers at the ice cream shop. Ryan's went on a large public notice board by the tourist information office, while Claire put hers up at the marina.

When they were done they rode back toward home, stopping at each house to deliver the flyers. Most of the people were amazed to hear that Opera Island was for sale and they promised to make a donation and to attend the fundraising barbecue on the weekend. At some houses there was nobody home and they had to just leave the flyer in the mailbox, or tuck it under the door.

After an hour or so they found themselves riding down a dirt side road. It looked vaguely familiar to Kendra.

"Hey, isn't this the way to Hackett Beach?" she said, suddenly remembering.

"That's right," said Claire. "And old Mrs. Simpson's house." The previous summer they had visited Mrs. Simpson to try and find more information about the sunken boat they were searching for. She lived in a spooky old house on the beach, filled with strange things that had washed up on the beach over the many years she had lived there.

As they turned into the driveway, a big black dog rushed out toward them, barking loudly. The last time he had terrified them, but this time they knew better.

"Hey, Charlie," called out Nathan, getting off his bike and holding his hand out to the dog. Charlie stopped and looked at him suspiciously, then walked over, his tail wagging.

"Charlie, what's all that noise about?" a voice called from the veranda of the house. An old woman stood in the doorway. She gave a whistle and Charlie obediently trotted back toward her and disappeared into the house.

"Hi, Mrs. Simpson," called Claire. "It's Claire Daniels, from down the road."

"Hello Claire," the woman answered. "And that must be your brother and your cousins if I remember correctly. What brings you here? Not searching for more wrecks, are you?"

"No, we're here to save Opera Island."

"Why, is it sinking?" She smiled and beckoned them onto the veranda. As they came up the stairs, Kendra noticed that some new beach treasures had been added to the collection. There was a beat-up yellow life jacket she didn't remember, and a wooden sign covered with Japanese writing.

Claire handed her a flyer and explained about the island being put up for sale. Mrs. Simpson shook her head as she read the flyer.

"They should never have automated that lighthouse," she said. "Those lighthouse keepers play an important role in keeping mariners safe. And if they still had a keeper, they wouldn't be putting the lighthouse up for sale." She sighed. "I don't get out as much these days, so I'm not sure I'll make it to your barbecue. But I will send in a donation. I hope you can manage to raise the money in time."

The children thanked her and made to leave. As she was about to go down the steps, Kendra asked about the new items on the veranda.

"A lot of stuff has been coming in from the Japanese tsunami," said Mrs. Simpson. "Both that street sign and the life jacket came from Japan. I heard somebody up the coast found a motorcycle, although I haven't found anything that big yet."

She ducked into the house briefly and came back holding a dirty looking soccer ball. "I just found this yesterday. It's from Japan as well." She spun the ball around and they could see Japanese writing on the side. "I might see if I can get this stuff translated to see where it came from."

They gazed at the soccer ball with its strange writing. Kendra wondered what it might say. A name, or an address, perhaps. Her grandfather lived in Japan, but luckily he was not affected by the earthquake or tsunami that had occurred a few years earlier. She resolved to ask him more about it next time they spoke.

Waving goodbye, they continued down the road. The next house had a very long driveway that wound its way through the trees until it emerged in front of a large modern house. The house was all black and grey, with metal siding and huge glass windows. A four-car garage stood off to the side. It couldn't be any more different from Aunt Jennie and Uncle William's house, thought Ryan as he got off his bike and leaned it against a tree.

A short, balding man with small steel-rimmed glasses answered the door when they knocked. He glanced at the flyer and then looked at Claire carefully as she explained about Opera Island.

"Hey, aren't you the kids that stopped those art thieves last summer?" he said when she had finished.

Claire nodded.

A big smile broke out across the man's face. "Well, I owe you a big thank you! One of those pieces was mine. I was heartbroken when it was stolen," he continued, "it's such a beautiful picture, I couldn't bear to live without it. Yet I thought I'd never see it again."

The man looked like he was ready to cry, just thinking about it. The four children stood there, not sure what to say.

"Would you like to see it?" he asked.

"Yes, please!" they answered together. They were all anxious to see this beautiful piece of art the man obviously felt so strongly about.

He led them through the house to the living room, which had high ceilings and a magnificent view over the ocean. Like the exterior, the inside walls and furniture were black and grey as well. The man pointed proudly toward the wall and they stopped and stared in amazement.

Mounted on the wall was a huge photograph. It covered most of the wall and was brightly lit from behind like a billboard. But what amazed them most was the subject of the photo. It appeared to be a parking lot, with a derelict looking car parked in it and some garbage strewn about.

"What do you think?" said the man, cocking his head to one side as he gazed at his picture.

"Ahh … it's very impressive," said Claire, choosing her words carefully. The others just nodded.

The man led them back to the front door. He promised to make a large donation to the campaign, partly as a thank you for rescuing his artwork.

They rode in silence for a few minutes, until they were well away from the house. Then they burst out laughing.

"Why would anyone want a picture of a parking lot in their house?" said Kendra in bewilderment.

No one knew.

"It must be worth a lot of money though," said Ryan. "Look at the house it's in."

"Maybe we could sell photos of parking lots to raise money for Opera Island," said Nathan. "It might raise more money than selling raffle tickets!"

They didn't see any more houses until they reached the end of the road. There, tucked into the trees, stood a small tumbledown cottage.

Tucked into the trees stood a tumbledown cottage.

Its roof was covered in moss, and the porch steps were crooked and uneven. It looked almost abandoned, but they could see a light on inside. Claire felt a bit of trepidation as they knocked on the door.

There were footsteps and the door slowly opened. Standing inside was a wizened old man, wearing blue overalls and a red flannel shirt. His back was stooped and he was no taller than Claire. But his eyes were bright and his voice lively as he said hello.

Claire began to explain what they were doing, but he stopped her short as soon as she mentioned Opera Island.

"For sale! Well, I'll be!" he said. "I used to live there, you know."

"On Opera Island?" said Ryan, surprised.

"Yes, I was the last lighthouse keeper. Ned McCaffrey's my name. The last of a long and proud line. That lighthouse was staffed by a dozen different keepers, of which I was the final one before they automated it. Now it's just some flashing lights run by a computer," he said, shaking his head sadly.

"Wow! What was it like being a lighthouse keeper?" said Kendra. "Was it lonely?"

"At times," he said with a shrug. "Some keepers go a bit crazy out there. Especially in the old days, when they used mercury in the lights. But it's an interesting life if you don't mind being alone. And you can't get a house with a better view anywhere! Anyway," he continued, "what's this about it being for sale?"

Claire finished telling him about the upcoming sale and the campaign to save the island and its lighthouse.

"It's a lot of money, but we think we can do it," she said. "Although I still don't know why anyone else would want to pay so much for it."

"Yes, it's pretty much just a pile of rocks and a lot of bird poop," the old man agreed. Then he laughed.

"Unless, of course, they're after the treasure!"

Books and More Books

"Treasure!" the four exclaimed together. "What treasure?"

"Oh, I don't think it's real," said Ned. "There was always a rumour among the lighthouse keepers that there was a fortune hidden somewhere on the island. I think it started because one of the old keepers, a man named Henry Cooper, always seemed to have more money to spend than seemed reasonable on a lighthouse keeper's salary."

The children exchanged looks. "Henry Cooper was the lighthouse keeper when the *Alexandria* sank," said Ryan, thinking back to the newspaper article they had read in the museum.

"That's right," replied the old man. "I believe he was quite a hero at the time, for all the lives he saved. But my father, who was also a lighthouse keeper before me, said that he had a reputation as an unpleasant character, and people around here didn't like him much. Maybe that's where the rumours about his fortune came from—people tend to spread rumours about those they don't like. He never married and he lived on Opera Island until he died in 1924."

"If he really did have a treasure, maybe that's why someone wants to buy the island," said Kendra.

"Well, I lived on that island for fourteen years, and I never found any treasure. My house wouldn't look like this if I had!" He laughed, and gave the door frame a thump with his fist, causing a small shower of paint flakes to flutter to the ground. "I'm afraid it's just an old story, kids."

The four children looked disappointed.

"Cheer up. Treasure or not, the island is worth saving. It's an important nesting ground, and the lighthouse is a piece of history. I'll be sure to come out to your barbecue on Saturday."

"That would be great, thanks Mr. McCaffrey," said Ryan. "By the way, do you know why it's called Opera Island?"

The old man smiled. "You know, I don't. You'd think I would, having lived there. When I was a little kid, my dad used to say it was because of the mermaids in the sea, who would sing opera for the lighthouse keepers. I liked that story so much that I never bothered to find out the real reason."

Ryan thanked him and they returned to their bikes. There were no more houses to canvass, so the children cycled back to the main road. When they turned toward home, Claire remembered they had to go back into Maple Harbour to pick up the remaining flyers.

"But I'm starving!" groaned Nathan.

"You can go home if you want," said Claire. "We can pick up the flyers."

"Or we could stop at Beth's for a cinnamon bun," suggested Kendra.

"That's a better idea," said Nathan. "I'd like to go to the library as well."

They rode the short distance back to the village, stopping to pick up the flyers at the print shop. They leaned their bikes against the railing at Beth's Bakery, which was in a ramshackle old cottage that had been converted to a bakery many years ago. Kendra could smell fresh baking from outside, and she unconsciously licked her lips in anticipation. Every time she was in Maple Harbour she made sure to have one of Beth's delicious cinnamon buns, which were the best she had tasted.

Soon they were sitting outside the bakery, savouring the sticky, gooey cinnamon buns.

"Do you think there could be treasure hidden on Opera Island?" said Kendra, licking icing off her fingers.

"No, you heard what Ned said," said Ryan. "The island is tiny. If there was anything hidden there he would have found it after living there for fourteen years. Maybe one of the previous lighthouse keepers found it."

"Or more likely there never was a treasure," said Claire. "Rumours like that usually aren't true."

"I suppose you're right," said Kendra glumly. "But it would have been a good explanation for why someone would be willing to pay so much for the island, if they knew something nobody else knew."

"That's still a mystery," agreed Claire. "I wish we knew more about the company that's buying it."

"Are you guys done yet?" said Nathan impatiently. "I'm ready to go to the library." As usual, Nathan had wasted no time in devouring his cinnamon bun.

"Okay, okay," said Claire. "But before we can go to the library, we have to put up more posters." She pulled out some small posters that the printer had included with the flyers. "We should take these to each business in town and ask if we can put one in their window."

They divided the posters up amongst themselves and agreed to meet at the library when they were done. Each set off in a different direction, stopping at every store along the way. Although Maple Harbour was quite small, it still took a long time to visit all the businesses, as each owner wanted to know more about the island and the fundraising campaign.

Kendra arrived at the library first. She was glad Nathan had wanted to go there, as she was hoping to find a book herself. Ryan and Nathan arrived a few minutes later, followed by Claire. They went together into the library and Nathan disappeared immediately into the non-fiction section. Kendra followed behind him, while Ryan and Claire looked at books and magazines while they waited.

A short while later Kendra returned to where Claire was sitting, reading a magazine. "Could I borrow your library card?" she asked.

"Sure," said Claire, handing it to her. "What are you getting out?"

"Oh, just a book," she replied, taking the card and turning away.

Nathan staggered out from the non-fiction section carrying a huge stack of books. "Look what I've got," he said, dropping them onto a table next to Claire and Ryan. "All these books about lighthouses!"

Ryan picked one up and looked at it. It was titled *An Illustrated History of Lighthouses*. Another one was called *West Coast Lighthouses, 1850 – 1950.* There were a dozen or more books scattered on the table, all about lighthouses.

"Are you checking all of these out?" he asked.

"Yup."

"You can't carry all those home on your bike!" said Claire. "Especially this one." She picked up an enormous hardcover book that was a couple of inches thick.

After considerable protest, Nathan was convinced to leave the largest books behind and he signed out the rest. Kendra quietly joined them, returning the library card to Claire. Whatever book she had signed out was hidden in her backpack.

They cycled home slowly. It had been a busy morning and the hot sun was now beating down on them as they rode. Nathan balanced one of his books on his handlebars as he rode, calling out facts about lighthouses.

"The first known lighthouse was the Pharos in Alexandria, Egypt. It was built in the 3rd century BC, was over 100 metres high, and was one of the seven wonders of the ancient world…"

"The tallest lighthouse is in Saudi Arabia. It's 133 meters tall. That's about the height of a 36-storey building…"

"There are still 27 staffed lighthouses in British Columbia…"

With Nathan's lighthouse facts to pass the time, they soon found themselves back at Pirate Cove. Aunt Jennie was watering the flower boxes in front of the house when they rode in.

"Did you pick up the flyers and posters?" she asked.

Claire nodded and gave Aunt Jennie the remaining flyers. "We put all the posters up around the village and handed out quite a lot of the flyers."

"Thank you. The Scouts have offered to go around and hand out the rest of these," she said.

"How's the fundraising going?" asked Claire.

"Pretty well," said Aunt Jennie with a satisfied look. "We've had a number of large donations. Including one from a man who said something about you four visiting to look at his art?"

They laughed and described the giant photograph to Aunt Jennie.

"Well, beauty is in the eye of the beholder, I suppose."

There was nothing more Aunt Jennie wanted them to do that day, so they packed a picnic lunch and took it down to the beach. The rest of the afternoon was spent lazily, swimming in the ocean and warming themselves in the hot sun. They explored the beach for shells and beach glass, and played a long game of frisbee, jumping off the dock to catch it in mid-air. Even Meg participated, catching the Frisbee in her mouth before falling into the water with a big splash. Nathan spent much of the afternoon absorbed in his books about lighthouses, calling out bits of information until everyone was tired of hearing him. They all moved away and only Meg remained, her chin on his lap, listening attentively to everything he said.

It was only the sight of smoke from the barbecue and Nathan's rumbling stomach that finally drove them away from the beach. The sun was getting low in the sky as they made their way to the house for dinner.

That night they were all in bed early. Riding into Maple Harbour combined with a long afternoon in the hot sun had worn them out. Climbing into her bed in Claire's room, Kendra slid the book she had taken from the library out of her backpack and began to read. It was a book on sailing, and she hoped to improve her sailing skills by reading it. But she didn't want the others to know, so she hid it under the covers when Claire came in.

Claire wasn't thinking about sailing as she lay in bed, trying to fall asleep. Instead, her mind wandered to the mysterious company that had made an offer to buy Opera Island. Who owned it and what did they want to do with the island? And why hide behind a numbered company? She resolved to try and find out tomorrow.

~8~

The Dunk Tank

The next morning, they were just finishing breakfast when Aunt Jennie strode into the kitchen with a large envelope in her hand.

"Could you run into town and drop these documents with Doug Mitchell?" she said to Uncle William. "They're to set up a trust account for the Opera Island fundraising."

"I can do it Mom," said Claire quickly, before her father had a chance to answer. Mr. Mitchell was the father of the awful Mitchell twins, Matthew and Flint. But he was also a lawyer, and dropping off the documents would give Claire a chance to ask a few questions herself.

"Sure, if you'd like to," her mother replied. Uncle William looked relieved, as he already had a lot to do that morning preparing for the barbecue.

"We can go with you," said Nathan. "And get another cinnamon bun."

"Not so fast," said Uncle William. "I need your help with a project this morning." Ryan's ears perked up. He liked helping Uncle William with projects around the house.

"I'll just go on my own," said Claire. "It will be faster that way."

With the envelope in her backpack, she cycled into the village until she reached the clothing store on the main street. Next to it was a glass door that said *D. A. Mitchell – Solicitor* on the front. She leaned her bike against the building and opened the door. A flight of stairs led up to the lawyer's office. There was nobody at the reception desk, but she could see Mr. Mitchell in his office through the open door. She knocked gently on the front desk and he raised his head.

"Hello Claire," the solicitor said, getting out of his chair and coming to greet her. "Have you brought the documents from your mom?"

"Yes, here they are." She reached into her pack and drew out the envelope. She handed it to him.

"Thank you." He opened the envelope and looked over the papers briefly. Satisfied they were all in order, he put them back in the envelope.

"That's certainly a big fundraising challenge your mother has taken on. I hope she's successful."

"It seems to be going pretty well so far." Claire told him about distributing the posters and flyers, and that there had been quite a few large donations already.

"And there will be a big fundraising barbecue on Saturday," she added.

"Oh yes, we'll be there," said Mr. Mitchell. "I believe Matthew and Flint are going to be helping out."

Claire groaned inwardly. Having the Mitchell brothers there was likely to be no help at all.

"The boys have been very concerned about the sale of Opera Island," he went on. "They donated a big chunk of their pocket money to the fund and convinced their soccer team to donate half the proceeds from their last car wash. They've explored around the lighthouse a few times and I think they feel quite attached to it."

"That's great!" she said, struggling to keep the surprise from showing on her face. Maybe the twins weren't as bad as they seemed.

"Well, I won't keep you," said Mr. Mitchell. "You probably have other things to do. Thanks for bringing these documents by."

"Actually, I was wondering if I could ask you a question," said Claire hesitantly.

"Sure," said the lawyer, looking at her inquiringly.

"It's about the company that's put an offer in on Opera Island. Do you know anything about them or why they want it?"

"Not offhand. But I can try and look up any information that's available online for you." He went back to his office and sat down at his computer. Claire waited in the reception area. After a few minutes he printed off a page and brought it out to her.

"Not a lot here, I'm afraid. It's a private company, so they don't have to disclose much information." He handed her the sheet of paper.

Claire looked it over. The company name was just a number, followed by the word _Ltd_. There was an incorporation date, showing the company had only been formed a few months ago. The mailing address was a post office box number in the city. And there were two names listed as company directors—Owen Gates and Jonathan Cooper, both with addresses in the city.

"Thanks." Claire turned to go, and then paused. "By the way, do you know why it's called Opera Island?"

Mr. Mitchell scratched his head thoughtfully. "Hmm. I'm not sure that I do. Funny, I've lived here all my life, so you'd think I'd know something like that." He shrugged. "It was probably named after one of the early explorers or their crew. Although it's a funny name for a person."

Claire thanked the lawyer again and went back outside to her bike. She pedalled slowly home, puzzling over the information he had given her. Something was familiar about those director names, but she couldn't think what.

Suddenly she slammed on her brakes and came to a halt. Reaching into her pack she pulled out the sheet and looked at it again.

That's it! she thought excitedly. Jonathan Cooper. That's the same last name as the lighthouse keeper on Opera Island! The one who was there when the *Alexandria* sank!

* * *

Uncle William had kept Ryan, Kendra, and Nathan busy all morning, building the dunk tank for the weekend's barbecue. When Claire rode in, everyone was busy around a big green tank with a platform on the side. A heavy wooden plank, like a small diving board, extended over the tank. From the plank, a rope led to a round target on a stick, painted in colourful rings with a bullseye at the centre. Ryan was filling the tank with water from a garden hose to test it for leaks.

"What do you think?" said Uncle William to Claire as she stopped her bike in front of the tank.

"Wow, you built all this today?" she said.

"I had some pretty good helpers," said Uncle William, with a wink toward Ryan.

"Here's the sign, Uncle William," said Kendra, emerging from the garage with a freshly painted sign in her hands. It said DUNK TANK in bright red letters.

"Perfect," said Uncle William, taking it from her. "I'll just put it up and we're done."

He went to the back of the tank and climbed up a set of steps to the platform. Ryan turned off the water and pulled the hose out of the tank. Uncle William carefully edged out onto the wooden plank with the sign in one hand and a hammer and nails in the other.

"Don't fall in," said Nathan.

"I won't," said his father.

"What if the plank gives way and drops you in?" said Claire. "Isn't that what it's supposed to do?"

"Not unless someone hits the target." He looked at Nathan sternly. "Don't get any ideas."

They watched as he nailed the sign to the side of the platform and then sat back to admire it. They all clapped.

At that moment a large raven flew down and settled on the target. Uncle William eyed it warily. He began to ease himself carefully back off the plank.

Meg, who had been lying in the shade of the garage while this went on, suddenly spotted the raven. She scrambled to her feet and gave a loud bark. The raven, startled, flew up from its perch on the target, giving a push with its powerful legs as it went.

Uncle William's eyes opened wide as the plank gave way under him. With a strangled cry, he dropped into the tank with a loud splash. He emerged moments later, spluttering and shaking water from his head, the hammer still clutched in his hand.

"Yikes!" he roared. "It's freezing!"

The kids were doubled over in laughter, while Meg ran around them, barking happily. Aunt Jennie came out from the house to see what all the commotion was about and she joined in the laughter when she saw Uncle William climbing out of the tank dripping wet.

Uncle William dropped into the tank with a loud splash!

Claire went into the house and got some towels. "At least you know it works," she said, handing Uncle William a towel.

"I might need to adjust that trigger mechanism a bit," he said, wiping water off his face. "It seems a bit sensitive. And as for you," he added, pointing a finger at Meg, "no more chasing ravens!"

Meg just wagged her tail and gazed at him contentedly. Why would she stop chasing ravens when it caused so much fun?

~9~

The Lighthouse

That evening Claire filled the others in on what she had learned at the lawyer's office.

"So you think the mysterious buyer might be related to Henry Cooper, the lighthouse keeper at the time of the *Alexandria* sinking?" said Kendra.

Claire nodded her head. "Maybe."

Ryan looked skeptical. "I don't know. Cooper's a pretty common name. It could just be a coincidence."

"You could be right," Claire admitted. "But I think it's worth going back to the island to take a look around."

They agreed that would be a good plan and the next morning they were up early, eager to visit the island and lighthouse again. After breakfast they packed a lunch and snacks, along with plenty of drinks and some extra clothes in case the weather changed. Nathan brought along one of the books he'd taken out from the library, placing it in a waterproof bag so it wouldn't get wet.

It looked like it would be a beautiful day, with only a few scattered clouds in the sky. A light breeze fluttered the flag at the top of *Pegasus'* mast. They stowed the food and extra clothes in the hatch and pushed the sailboat into the water. Meg was the first one into the boat, curling herself into a ball in her usual spot near the bow. When they were all on board, they pushed away from the dock and set off for the island.

Ryan took the tiller and steered them out of the bay. He was glad to be on the water again, feeling the tug of the tiller in his hand and nudging it one way or the other to keep the sails filled with wind. He felt he was really becoming quite adept at sailing.

Kendra watched him from the front of the boat. She was happy to see Ryan enjoying himself, but she was frustrated at her own inability to sail well. Why couldn't it be as easy as everything else she tried? I guess this is how Ryan feels about most things, she thought to herself guiltily. She decided to let Ryan do the sailing that morning and she settled herself down next to Meg. She closed her eyes and listened to the gentle lapping of the waves against the side of the boat.

Nathan was reading from his book. Every so often he called out bits of information that he found interesting.

"The oldest lighthouse still standing is the Tower of Hercules in Spain. It was built by the Romans more than 1800 years ago…"

"The first lighthouses used wood fires for light. Then they switched to oil lamps, and now all of them use electric lights…"

"The oldest lighthouse in British Columbia is Fisgard Lighthouse on Vancouver Island. It was built in 1860 and is a National Historic Site…"

"Enough!" cried Claire. "If I hear one more lighthouse fact, I'm going to scream!"

"The light—" began Nathan, but Claire snatched the book out of his hand and only agreed to give it back once he promised to read to himself.

After an hour or so they arrived at Opera Island. Ryan steered them carefully around to the spot where they had pulled up previously. Meg recognized where they were and put her paws up on the side of the boat, wagging her tail excitedly. As soon as they touched the shore she hopped over and ran toward the lighthouse. She soon came back carrying the old rubber ball in her mouth.

Claire jumped out and tied the bow line to the post. She picked up the ball which Meg had dropped at her feet and threw it across the island. With a joyous little bark, Meg tore off after it.

"So what are we looking for?" said Ryan as he got out of the boat.

"I'm not really sure," Claire replied. "Anything unusual, I guess."

They walked over to the lighthouse and began to look around. As they had noted on their first visit to the island, both the main door to the lighthouse and the door to the attached building were securely locked.

"How are we supposed to find anything if we can't get inside?" said Nathan.

"Maybe there's a window we could climb in," suggested Kendra.

They walked all the way around the lighthouse, peering upward. But the only windows were at the very top of the lighthouse, and there was no way to scale its smooth stone walls.

They poked around the foundation of the old light keeper's house, but there was no basement or cellar or anything else of interest. Then they explored the rest of the island, but it was mostly just smooth rock, with no caves or hiding spots. All around them gulls swooped and cawed, wary of the intruders on their island.

By now it was getting hot and everyone was quite discouraged.

"Let's go for a swim," said Nathan. He picked up Meg's ball from the ground where she had dropped it and tossed it into the sea. Meg leapt into the water and began swimming after it. Nathan plunged in after her, quickly followed by the others. Kendra, who was the strongest swimmer, passed them all and reached the ball just ahead of Meg. She threw it toward the shore and Meg turned around to get it. Soon they were all throwing the ball back and forth between them, while Meg swam back and forth, barking.

"Poor Meg," said Claire. "It's not very fair, is it? You just can't doggy-paddle fast enough." She tossed the ball back on shore and Meg clambered out of the water. Shaking herself vigorously, she lay down in the sun and happily chewed on her ball.

The four children continued to splash about in the water until Nathan reminded them it was lunchtime and they all suddenly felt hungry. Kendra went to the boat and pulled out the lunch and drinks. They sat on the hot rocks and ate their sandwiches, water dripping off them. Aunt Jennie had given them a thermos of homemade lemonade, and they drank it thirstily. It was just the right mix of tartness and sweetness, perfect for a hot summer's day.

Meg got up and wandered over to them. She paused next to Kendra and dropped the dirty, saliva-covered ball into her lap.

"Ugh. That ball is gross, Meg," she said with disgust. She picked it up gingerly and hurled it away toward the lighthouse. The ball bounced a few times and then disappeared from sight. Meg took off after it.

"She'll just bring it back," said Claire with a laugh. But Meg didn't bring the ball back. She wandered back and forth a few times with her nose to the ground and then began to whimper and whine. After listening to her for a while, Nathan got up and went over. She looked up at him expectantly and then down at the ground in front of her. Nathan spied a crack in the rock, just wide enough for a ball to fit through. Nathan peered into it, but it was too dark to see very far and there was no sign of Meg's ball.

"Sorry, Meg. I think your ball is lost for good this time." Meg looked at him sadly. She remained by the crack, whimpering, as Nathan returned to his lunch. The others were discussing what to do next.

"If we had a rope we could climb up to the window," said Kendra.

"I have a rope on *Pegasus*, but it's not long enough," said Claire. "Besides, how would we get it up there?"

"What about picking the combination lock?" said Nathan. "We could try every combination until it opens."

"That would take us days," said Ryan. "There are thousands of possible combinations." He thought for a moment. "Unless …"

He jumped up and ran toward the lighthouse. The others looked at each other in surprise and then got up and followed him. Ryan went to the door of the shed and looked at the lock closely. Then he began to turn the numbers on the lock carefully, tugging gently as he went. The three children watched him, holding their breath.

Suddenly there was a click and the lock opened. With a cry of triumph, Ryan held it up in the air!

~10~

The Trap Door

How did you do that?" asked Nathan incredulously.

"Magic," replied Ryan, with a grin.

"No, really, how did you do it?' said Claire.

"I read somewhere that a lot of people are lazy and only change one of the dials on the lock. That way it's quicker for them to open. It's a bad idea because it's easy for thieves to open, but people still do it. So I thought I'd give it a try, just changing one dial at a time until it opened."

Ryan slowly opened the door. Inside it was dark, and particles of dust danced in the stream of sunlight coming through the door. He stepped into the room, followed by Claire. They looked around but it was hard to distinguish anything in the gloom.

"It's pretty dark in here," he said. "We're going to need a flashlight."

Nathan ran back to *Pegasus* to get a flashlight. He returned with one shortly and handed it to Ryan, who switched it on. The beam wasn't very strong.

"Sorry, I meant to get new batteries for that light," said Claire with a frown.

Although the light was dim, it was enough to see what was in the room. It was a storage shed, still filled with odds and ends. There were old tools, somewhat rusty, as well as tins of nails and screws, bits of wire, and an assortment of cans and bottles on the shelves. Meg, who had followed them in, sniffed at one of the old cans. Kendra picked it up and looked at it.

"This is just old paint," she said, putting it back on the shelf.

"This one says Engine Oil," said Nathan, reading from a label on an old bottle.

In one corner was a large barrel. Nathan lifted the lid but it was empty. Ryan shone the flashlight into each corner and up at the ceiling, but there wasn't much else to see.

At the other end of the room they could see the wall of the lighthouse. In the middle of the wall was another door. Ryan turned the handle and the door opened. He pushed it open and went through, followed by the others.

They were standing in an octagonal room with a wood floor covered with a thick layer of dust. Unlike the storage building, which had been hot and stuffy, the lighthouse itself was cool and pleasant, thanks to its thick concrete walls.

In the middle of the room was a spiral staircase, made of black metal. It disappeared through an opening in the floor above, leading to the top of the lighthouse. A faint light came down through the opening, allowing them to see.

"That must be the light room!" said Nathan excitedly, pointing upward. "Let's go check it out." He started up the steps.

"Wait a minute," said Claire, grabbing his arm. "How do we know this thing is safe?"

"It seems pretty sturdy," said Ryan, shaking the railing. "And it doesn't look rusted or broken," he added, shining the light on it.

"All right. But go slowly and test each step before you put your weight on it."

Nathan nodded. He slowly made his way up the staircase, checking each step with his foot as he went. When he reached the top he called down to them. "It's all okay. Come on up."

Kendra went next, followed by Ryan and Claire. As they climbed the stairs, they could hear Nathan exclaiming loudly from above.

"You'll have to stay down here Meg," said Claire, giving her a pat on the head. Meg obediently sat at the bottom of the staircase and watched dolefully as they disappeared out of view.

When they popped through the opening into the light room, they found themselves blinking in the bright sunlight. While the lower part of the lighthouse tower had no windows, the light room was completely surrounded by glass. There was an unobstructed view for miles in every direction. They could see boats of all shapes and sizes sprinkled across the sea like toys. Other islands lay off in the distance and behind them a line of sharp mountain peaks rose hazily in the distance.

"Wow, look at that view!" said Kendra.

"Never mind that. Look at this lens!" said Nathan.

In the middle of the room was a huge glass lens. It was nearly a metre high and made up of dozens of glass prisms. On each of its six sides there was a round piece of glass like a giant eye. The whole thing looked like a cross between an enormous lightbulb and a crystal chandelier.

"Is that the light?" asked Kendra.

"No, it's just the lens. The light goes inside, but it's not there anymore." He peered up into the lens from the bottom. The others crowded around to take a look.

"It's called a Fresnel lens," said Nathan. "It concentrates the light. It was invented in France in the 1800's and allowed lighthouses to be seen from far away." Nathan pointed to some gears and a metal track the lens was mounted on. "That's how they rotated the lens."

"Why does it need to rotate?" asked Ryan.

"To make it flash."

"You mean the light doesn't just turn on and off?"

"No, the lens rotates and it looks like its flashing when the prisms line up."

When they had all examined the lens, they looked about the room. But other than the lens, it was completely empty.

"Nowhere to hide anything here," said Claire, shaking her head. She started back down the steps. Ryan followed her, while Kendra and Nathan remained in the light room. Meg was waiting for them at the bottom, wagging her tail eagerly. She didn't like to be left behind.

Claire and Ryan examined the room at the bottom of the lighthouse. It was mostly empty as well. There was a cardboard box tucked under the back of the staircase and Claire went to take a look. As she did, she stumbled over something on the floor.

Catching herself, she bent down to take a look. Her fingers touched something hard and cold. Ryan shone the flashlight down on the floor. Brushing away the dust and dirt, she saw what looked like a round steel handle. Brushing further, she exposed a thin crack running across the floor in either direction.

"It's a trap door!" said Ryan excitedly.

Claire grabbed the handle and pulled. She felt it give a little, but it was too heavy. Ryan bent over and grabbed the handle as well. Together they were able to lift the heavy trap door. Pulling it all the way up, it fell against the back wall with a bang.

"What was that?" shouted Kendra from the top of the staircase.

"We found a trap door!" called up Claire.

"It leads to some sort of cellar," said Ryan, pointing the flashlight down to reveal more stairs. The light was getting very dim now, barely penetrating the gloom.

There was a clatter of footsteps as Kendra and Nathan rushed down to join them. They peered down through the opening.

"Cool! A secret hiding spot!" said Nathan.

"It's not really secret," said Claire. "If the floor wasn't so dirty we'd have seen it easily."

"Still, it's probably where you'd hide something if you wanted to hide something," said Kendra.

"Who's going first?" asked Ryan, looking at Claire. She shrugged and took the flashlight from him. But Meg, who had been peering through the hole with them, suddenly pushed past her and scurried down the steps to the bottom, disappearing into the darkness.

"I guess Meg's going first!" laughed Kendra.

Claire followed after Meg, but going more slowly and carefully as it was very difficult to see anything. When she reached the bottom she shone the light on the steps so the others could find their way down. When they all stood together in the cellar, she shone the light around.

The cellar was cold and damp. They were disappointed to see that it was as empty as all the other rooms in the lighthouse. There were some empty wooden boxes, but nothing else. The floor of the room was wet, adding to the gloom. Unlike the rest of the lighthouse, the walls in this room were made of old wood panels. Hooks and nails were placed in the walls at various places, and on one side there was an empty set of shelves. But there was nothing else to see.

"Nothing here," said Ryan glumly. They all felt discouraged. There were no more rooms to search, and they'd found nothing of interest. Nathan started back up the stairs. He wanted to look at that lens again before they had to go.

"What's Meg sniffing at?" said Kendra, pointing to the corner of the room. Meg had her nose to the bottom of the wall and was sniffing vigorously. She began to whine and whimper as she sniffed. Then she stepped back, stared at the wall, and barked.

Claire walked over and pointed the flashlight at the wall where Meg was looking.

"There's nothing there, Meg, you silly dog," she said, shining the light back and forth.

"Meg's not a silly dog, she's a smart dog," said Nathan indignantly. He came back down the stairs and put his arms around Meg's neck. "If she says there's something there, then there probably is."

"There's a knothole in the wood," said Kendra. She bent down and looked at it. Then she stuck her finger through it.

"Don't let it bite you," said Ryan.

Kendra hurriedly pulled her finger back out, but when she saw Ryan laughing she put it back through the hole and felt around.

"I can touch something," she said. "It feels like a hook." She could feel something curved beneath the knothole, so she hooked her finger around it and tugged. It pulled upward and as it did she felt the knothole move slightly. She gave another tug, and the others stared in amazement as an entire section of the wood panelling pulled out toward her, pivoting in the middle. She pulled it open further and then stepped back so Claire could shine the flashlight in.

Behind the wall was a narrow cave leading into the rock. And, sitting on the floor of the cave, was Meg's ball!

Kendra Shares a Secret

Meg gave a joyous bark and picked up her ball. She displayed it proudly, wagging her tail.

"You clever dog, Meg," said Kendra. "You've discovered a secret cave!" Everyone crowded around to congratulate Meg, patting her on the head.

Claire shone the light around the cave. It wasn't very big, perhaps the size of a small car. But it went quite far back, although it began to get very narrow further in. There seemed to be a very weak light coming from the far end.

"The cave must lead to the crack in the rocks where Meg's ball fell in!" said Nathan.

"And that's why the floor is all wet," said Ryan. "Rain can fall into that crack as well."

"Let's explore and see what's in there!" said Kendra.

Claire took one step toward the entrance. But at that moment the flashlight, which had become very dim, flickered and went out completely. They were left standing in the dark.

Claire groaned. She shook the flashlight and flicked the switch back and forth, but nothing happened. She peered into the cave, but it was pitch black except for the faint light at the back.

"We'll have to come back with fresh batteries," she said. Claire could sense everyone's disappointment, even though she couldn't see their faces in the dark. "It's okay, we can come back tomorrow. It's too late to make it back today."

Reluctantly, she swung the wood panel closed and Kendra felt around in the knothole until she located the hook again. This time she pushed it down until it slid into place, locking the secret door once more.

They could just see their way out of the cellar by the light coming through the hatch. Carefully, they made their way up the steps, through the storage room, and out. Ryan locked the door with the combination lock, taking care to turn all the numbered dials so that no one else could open it as easily as he had. They gathered their things and put them back in *Pegasus*. Nathan untied them and pushed off. Meg lay at the front, chewing happily on her ball. They hadn't the heart to make her leave it behind again after rediscovering it.

There was a strong breeze and *Pegasus* sped through the water, waves foaming around the bow. Every so often a larger wave broke against the bow and showered them in spray, causing shrieks of laughter. They didn't mind the cold water, as it was a very hot day. Ryan was at the tiller, making neat tacks back and forth toward Pirate Cove.

"Do you want to steer, Kendra?" he asked after they were about halfway home.

She hesitated a moment. "No thanks."

"Come on, you should take a turn," said Claire. Kendra just shook her head and looked the other way. Claire looked at her questioningly, and then at Ryan, who just shrugged.

Nathan's stomach told him it was getting close to dinner time as they drew up to the wharf in Pirate Cove. They pulled *Pegasus* up on the dock and stored the lifejackets and other equipment in the shed. From the stairs they could see Uncle William on the back deck standing at the barbecue. Clouds of smoke were pouring out and Uncle William was waving it away from his face with one hand while he moved hamburgers about with the other. He gave them a wave as he saw them come up.

Inside Aunt Jennie was making a salad. She quickly gave them each a task; cutting up vegetables, finding the condiments, and setting the table outside. Soon they were all sitting down on the back deck munching on hamburgers.

"So, you went back to Opera Island to look around?" said Uncle William. "Did you find anything interesting?"

"Not too much," said Claire quickly. That was sort of true—they hadn't found anything yet.

"Meg found a ball," said Nathan, glancing at the others. Kendra bit into her hamburger to hide a smile.

"But we'd like to go back again tomorrow," said Claire.

"Don't forget about the big fundraising barbecue tomorrow," Aunt Jennie said.

"Oh no," groaned Claire. "Do we all have to go?"

"Yes, we need all the help we can get," said her mother, giving her a surprised look. "I thought you'd be looking forward to it!"

"We are," said Ryan. "But we also wanted to go back to the island."

"You could go after the barbecue is finished," said Uncle William as he helped himself to more salad.

"Yes," said Aunt Jennie. "There will still be plenty of time. You can pack a dinner and take it with you. Just make sure you're home well before dark."

Claire nodded. That would do. "We can sail *Pegasus* into Maple Harbour in the morning," she said. "Then we can leave directly from there."

Having settled on a plan, they finished up their dinner. Aunt Jennie had baked a rhubarb pie for dessert. Kendra laughed in spite of herself. When they had visited earlier that summer Aunt Jennie had been trying to use up all the rhubarb she had been given by a neighbour.

"You still have rhubarb left?" she said to Aunt Jennie.

"Yes, the freezer is still full of it, I'm afraid," she said.

"I don't mind," said Ryan, helping himself to another piece of pie.

After dinner, Uncle William and Aunt Jennie kept them busy getting things ready for the fundraiser. There were plates, cutlery, cups, and napkins to be loaded into boxes. Raffle tickets needed to be organized and numbers recorded. And Uncle William's dunk tank needed to be drained and taken apart so it could be transported into the village. It was dark by the time they finished.

After getting ready for bed, Claire and Kendra were too excited to fall asleep. It was going to be a busy day tomorrow, with both the barbecue and another trip to Opera Island. And this time with sufficient lights to explore the secret cave.

After trying to read for a while, Claire put her book down and looked over at Kendra. "What are you reading?" she asked.

"Nothing," said Kendra, tucking the book under the covers.

But Claire had already seen it. "Is that a book about sailing?" Kendra nodded her head.

"Does that have anything to do with why you didn't want to steer today?"

Kendra nodded again. Then she reluctantly explained how frustrated she'd been at her inability to figure out sailing. And how hurt she'd felt when Ryan took over from her the previous day.

"I've never found anything to be this hard to learn before," she complained.

Claire laughed. "That's not a bad problem to have. If sailing is the only thing you're not so good at." Then, more seriously, she said, "You know, you don't have to be really good at something to enjoy it. I'm awful at painting, but I still like to do it."

"I know," said Kendra. "But I still find it hard."

"Well, the only way to get better is to practise more. Reading a book is fine, but real learning happens on the water. If you want, tomorrow you can be the one to take us to Opera Island. Don't worry about being perfect, just practise. And have fun. I'll make sure to give you some tips to help out."

"Okay," said Kendra, "thanks." She pulled the book out from under the covers. "I guess I don't need to read this anymore tonight. Because it's kind of boring." She made a face and they both laughed.

Kendra closed the book and placed it on the night table. Then she pulled up the covers and closed her eyes. Within minutes both girls were fast asleep.

~12~

The BBQ

The next morning Uncle William woke them up early. "Come on sleepyheads. There's a lot to do today."

One by one they emerged from their bedrooms, rubbing their eyes.

"Get yourself some breakfast," said Aunt Jennie. "And then you can start loading things into the truck."

At the mention of breakfast, Nathan perked up. Aunt Jennie had fried some bacon and eggs, which they helped themselves to along with thick slices of toast and jam. As soon as they finished eating, Uncle William was ready to go.

"I need two of you to come with me in the truck and help me unload it," he said. "Then we'll go pick up some tables and chairs for the barbecue."

"Can we all come?" asked Kendra.

"I can only fit two in the truck," he replied.

"Ryan, why don't you and Nathan go?" said Claire. "Kendra and I can sail around in *Pegasus*."

It was agreed that the boys would go with Uncle William while the girls sailed into the village. Ryan and Nathan helped Uncle William load the last few boxes into the truck and then they climbed in and drove off.

Claire and Kendra washed up the dishes and then made preparations for sailing into Maple Harbour.

"We'll need to bring some food for dinner," said Claire, "since it will be past dinner by the time we get back."

"Yes, we don't want Nathan grumbling about his stomach the whole time!" said Kendra with a laugh.

They made some sandwiches and put them in a cooler bag, along with some leftover potato salad, a few apples, some cookies, and a bag of potato chips. They also packed some sweaters in case it got cool in the evening, and an extra flashlight along with spare batteries.

When they were finished packing, they carried the gear down to the dock, followed closely by Meg. They slid the loaded boat into the water and set off. Claire indicated to Kendra that she should steer.

"I thought this would be a good opportunity for you to get a bit more practice," she said.

Kendra was a little nervous after their discussion last night. But she remembered what Claire had said about practising and having fun. She moved to the back of the boat and took the tiller. She steered them out of the cove, the light wind blowing gently from the side. As they came out into the strait, she turned into the wind as Claire pulled in the sail. *Pegasus* moved swiftly through the water.

Kendra began to relax. She liked the feeling of the wind blowing her hair around, and she felt less nervous without Ryan and Nathan in the boat watching her. Claire gave her a few tips and suggestions, helping her keep the little boat on a smooth and even course. After a while she decided to tack and, calling out a warning to Claire, turned the boat through the wind. Claire smiled and nodded approvingly as she brought them up to speed in the other direction.

They tacked back and forth along the coast toward Maple Harbour. With each turn, Kendra gained confidence. By the time they approached the village, she felt like she had finally figured this sailing thing out.

"Okay, sail in there," said Claire, pointing at the harbour entrance.

Kendra looked at her in surprise. "Oh, no. I think you'd better bring it into the dock."

Claire shook her head. "You can do it. Just keep doing what you've been doing."

Doubts flooded back to Kendra. Sailing in the wide open strait with nothing around to run into was one thing, but she wasn't sure she was ready for the close confines of the marina. There were too many other boats around, and worse, all sorts of people watching her.

She took a deep breath and pointed *Pegasus* toward the harbour entrance. As they came past the breakwater she saw a large power boat coming in the other direction.

"Just keep to this side," said Claire calmly. She let the sail out so they were barely moving. The other boat passed them slowly, the owner giving a wave as he went by. Claire waved back, but Kendra was too focused on where she was steering to notice. Before she knew it they were approaching the public wharf. The wind was very light inside the harbour and they nosed gently up to the dock. Claire hopped out, holding the rope.

"You see, no problem!" said Claire.

Kendra flushed with pride. She didn't say anything in response but gave Meg a big hug when they were all up on the dock. "I did it Meg!" she whispered in the dog's ear, who licked her face in response.

When they reached the park where the barbecue was to be held, it was bustling with activity. People were setting up tables and stalls and games and activities. Smoke was beginning to billow from a line of barbecues set up in the middle. They spotted Uncle William's truck on the other side. Ryan and Nathan were busy unloading tables and chairs.

"Good, you're here," said Ryan. "You can help us move these over there." He pointed to a spot near the barbecues.

Claire and Kendra got to work moving the tables and chairs, and then helped set them up. They were just finishing when the first people started to arrive. Aunt Jennie hurried over to them.

"Here's the raffle tickets, and some money to make change." She handed them each a roll of raffle tickets and a cloth bag to hold the money. "We need you to sell a lot of tickets, so get started." And with that she was off.

They decided to split up and work in pairs. Kendra and Nathan set off in one direction while Claire and Ryan went in the other.

Selling raffle tickets was a good job to have, thought Ryan, as they wandered about the park. It was pleasant walking about in the shade of the trees, and people were happy to buy tickets from them. As the day wore on, more people arrived and it began to get busier. It also got hotter. Perhaps it wasn't as easy a job as he'd thought.

"Let's get a drink," he said to Claire. They saw a sign for cold drinks and walked over to the booth. Claire stopped short.

"That's the Mitchell brothers," she said under her breath. "I'm not buying anything from them."

"Don't be silly," said Ryan. "We're just buying a drink." He walked up to the booth and asked for an iced tea. Flint Mitchell handed it to him and then looked over at Claire.

"Hi, Claire. What would you like?"

Claire looked at him suspiciously and pointed to a can of lemonade sitting in a large cooler of ice water.

"Here you go," he said, handing her the can.

"Good luck with the raffle tickets," said Matthew Mitchell as they were leaving.

"They seem a lot nicer than usual," said Ryan.

"I suppose so," muttered Claire. The twin brothers had been unusually friendly. She recalled what their dad had said about them raising funds for Opera Island. And now they were here helping out with the barbecue. It did seem like they were turning over a new leaf. Claire still had her doubts though.

Rather than buying drinks, Kendra and Nathan had stopped to buy mini donuts, as Nathan was hungry again. They watched the little donuts float down a river of hot oil in a miniature assembly line, before being scooped into a bag and dusted with sugar.

"Mmm," said Nathan, popping three in his mouth at once. "I love these!"

They wandered over to the dunk tank, where a large crowd had gathered. A large man in a suit, with a string of medallions around his neck, was sitting on the platform above the tank.

"That's the mayor," said Nathan.

"Why is he wearing all those funny medals?" Kendra asked.

Nathan shrugged. "I've no idea, but he always wears them." He grinned. "Maybe he really wants to be a rap star!"

There was a line of people waiting to throw balls at the target, hoping to drop the mayor into the tank. But they all missed. Finally, a small boy, only three or four years old, approached the tank with a ball in his hand. The mayor seemed confident that he was going to escape a dunking, but the little boy hit the target right in the middle. The mayor went down with a howl and a splash, to thunderous applause from the watching crowd.

Aunt Jennie saw them and came over.

"How are the raffle ticket sales?" she asked.

"Pretty good," said Kendra, showing her the tickets they'd sold. "How is the rest of the fundraising going?"

"Really well. It's even busier than I expected. And people are making a lot of donations. So I think we're well on our way to raising the money we need!"

"Will you have to go in the dunk tank?" asked Nathan.

Aunt Jennie grimaced. "I suppose so." She hadn't anticipated that being on the village council would involve being dropped in cold water!

"Good," said Nathan. "Let us know so we can watch!"

"At least it's hot out," said Kendra sympathetically. She thought it would be fun to go in the dunk tank. But she could tell her aunt didn't agree.

The four of them continued to sell raffle tickets the rest of the day, stopping only for a short lunch break. They saw many of the same people they had delivered the flyers to, including the old lighthouse keeper and the man with the strange art in his house.

Sophie, the museum curator, was hosting a table covered in artifacts from the museum. The handliner rowboat they had seen there was on display in front of the table and a large crowd had gathered to admire it. Kendra and Nathan ran into the printer, who was much friendlier than he'd been when they saw him in the print shop.

"All those flyers you handed out must have done their job," he remarked. "It seems like everybody in the village is here!"

Finally, the barbecue came to an end. Aunt Jennie gave a short speech to the crowd, thanking them for their support and confirming that they had raised enough money to save Opera Island!

Everybody cheered.

"All right, let's go," said Claire as the crowd began to disperse.

"Not so fast," said Uncle William, who had snuck up behind them. "We need to clean up now."

The children groaned.

Uncle William put them to work packing up the tables and chairs and loading them into the truck. It was harder work in the hot afternoon sun than setting them up that morning had been. The four of them wiped the sweat from their brows as they loaded the last table into the truck. They moved into the shade of a tall, stone retaining wall at the edge of the park, and drank some water. Meg, who had rejoined them after spending the afternoon looking for hot dogs that had dropped on the ground, flopped down in the shade, panting.

"Can we go now?" asked Nathan.

"I think so," said Claire. "Everything seems to be taken down. But maybe we'll just check with mom and dad."

Suddenly they heard giggling above them. They looked up and saw Mathew Mitchell's head peeking over the top of the retaining wall before it was quickly pulled back.

"What are you two up to?" said Claire suspiciously.

Almost before the words were out of her mouth, the two boys were back, holding the cooler of ice water from the drink stand between them. They tipped it over and a shower of ice and freezing water came hurtling down!

A shower of ice and freezing water came hurtling down!

~13~

Back to Opera Island

The four children leaped back just in time to avoid getting soaked. But poor Meg was not as lucky. The flood of icy cold water landed right on her back. Startled, she leapt to her feet and looked around in surprise. Then she shook herself violently, spraying water all around and covering the four children in a shower of water droplets. They shrieked as the cold spray hit them.

"Meg, stop that!" cried Kendra. But Meg continued to shake, water flying in all directions.

Above, the Mitchell brothers howled with laughter as they ran away from the scene.

"Poor Meg," said Ryan when the dog finally stopped shaking. But Meg didn't seem too unhappy about being doused in cold water. In fact, since it was a very hot day, she had quite liked it.

"So much for the Mitchells being nicer," muttered Claire to Ryan. He nodded his head in agreement.

Nathan wanted to chase after the two boys, but Claire insisted they get going.

"We still need to get to Opera Island to explore that cave," she said. "And I need to stop at the marina and get a new pin for the mast. The old one's coming loose."

The marina store was a short distance from the park, so they walked over together. The store was in a small, white-washed building near the water. Colourful flags and pennants hung around the edge of the roof, fluttering in the wind. They pushed open the door, causing a door chime to sound softly.

Inside, the store was filled with marine gear. To Claire this was better than being in a candy store. Her eyes roamed the shelves of pulleys and cleats, the reels full of ropes and cables, and the expensive navigation equipment in glass cabinets. At the back of the store, George, the store owner, was talking to a thin man with short dark hair. George pointed to a wall with maps and safety equipment and the man thanked him and went over to look.

"Hi kids," said George. "How was the barbecue? Your dad dropped by to get some rope and told me you were selling raffle tickets."

"I think it went pretty well," said Claire. "Mom seems happy with the fundraising effort. She thinks we'll have enough to buy the island."

"We're going there right now!" said Nathan excitedly. "We think we might have found …"

Claire elbowed him sharply and Nathan stopped
mid-sentence. She glanced toward the man by the
wall. He seemed to be engrossed in the maps, but she
thought she'd seen him stiffen when Opera Island
was mentioned. Claire hurriedly asked George about
the pin she was looking for. He went to the back of
the shop to look, returning a few minutes later.

"This should work," he said, handing it to her.

Claire thanked him. She paid for the pin and they
left. As soon as they were outside, she turned to
Nathan furiously.

"Nathan! You nearly gave it away!"

"What did I do?" complained Nathan. "It's just
George, he's our friend."

"Yes, but what about that other guy who was in
the store?"

At that moment the door opened and the thin
man stepped out. He walked past them without a
glance and strode off toward the parking lot.

"What does it matter?" said Nathan when the
man was out of earshot. "It's just somebody buying a
map. He's not interested in what we found."

"Let's hope not," grumbled Claire.

They watched as the man got into a convertible sports car and pulled out of the parking lot. Ryan watched as it drove away. The car had a personalized vanity licence plate, with the number 0H1 G8S. He puzzled over it for a moment. Usually personalized license plates had a person's name or some other words related to who they were, but he couldn't make any sense of this one.

"Come on, let's go," said Claire. They walked back over to the park. Aunt Jennie was speaking to a man standing next to a black car. As they approached, the man got back in his car and drove away. Claire recognized him as Pete Saunders, the real estate agent. Aunt Jennie had a worried look on her face.

"What's wrong?" asked Kendra.

Aunt Jennie sighed. "Pete just told me that there has been an increase in the offer to buy Opera Island. It's quite a bit higher than before, and it's more money than we have." She sounded quite despondent.

The faces of the four children fell.

"Can we raise more money?" said Ryan.

"The sale closes at midnight tonight," said Aunt Jennie gloomily. "I'll try, but I'm not holding out much hope."

"We're sailing to Opera Island now," said Claire.

Her mother nodded. "It may be your last chance to do so," she said. "Just make sure you're back before dark."

"We will," they promised, and set off for the public wharf where *Pegasus* was tied up.

"Now we *have* to find that treasure, if it exists," said Nathan as they made their way to the wharf.

"I don't understand," said Kendra. "Even if we find a hidden fortune, how will that stop the sale of the island?"

"We can use it to buy the island!" said Nathan.

"Sort of, but not exactly," said Claire. "Any fortune on the island would belong to the current owner, which is the federal government. But if we find it, then maybe they'll stop the sale. Or the buyers won't be interested anymore, since the government would keep the treasure."

"The first thing we need to do is find out if there's anything there," said Ryan. "Then we can worry about what will happen."

Walking through the marina parking lot toward the wharf, Ryan noticed the expensive convertible with the vanity licence plate again. He looked around, and saw the thin man near the boat rental outlet, speaking with the operator. He nudged Claire and pointed.

"It's probably just a coincidence," she said. But she looked concerned.

Ryan looked again at the car's licence plate. It bothered him that he couldn't understand its meaning. Usually he was pretty good at puzzles.

Pegasus was where Kendra and Claire had left it that morning, bobbing gently in the water. Meg hopped in immediately and settled into the bow. Nathan pulled up the sail and Ryan untied the rope holding them to the dock.

"Okay, let go," said Claire. But Ryan held onto the rope. He was staring back toward the parking lot.

"Let go!" said Claire impatiently. "What are you waiting for?"

Still Ryan held onto the rope. He turned toward her, his mouth open in surprise.

"I've got it!" he said. "The licence plate! It's Owen Gates!" The others looked at him blankly. "0H1 G8S. Owen Gates! The other director of the numbered company!"

14

Trapped!

"**I** get it!" said Nathan excitedly. "Oh-1 is Owen and G8 is Gate, with an S on the end!"

"And that's the other name that was on the list of directors for the company buying Opera Island!" said Claire.

"Right," said Ryan, nodding his head vigorously. "And now he's here, renting a boat!"

"Do you think he's going to Opera Island right now?" said Kendra.

"Probably. Now he knows we've discovered something," said Claire, giving Nathan a scowl. Nathan opened his mouth to respond but then thought better of it. He had a sinking feeling that Claire might be right. Maybe he had given everything away.

Claire looked back toward the boat rental outlet. The operator had gone back inside and the thin man was walking toward his car, his hands in his pockets. She looked at the dock in front of the rental outlet. A smile formed on her face.

"He won't be going to Opera Island just yet," she said. "All the boats are rented."

The others looked over at the rental dock. All the berths were empty.

"Let's go then!" said Ryan. "Before someone brings a boat back." He tossed the rope he was holding into *Pegasus* and pushed them away from the wharf before hopping in. Nathan paddled them away while Kendra steered. Soon they were out of the marina and heading for Opera Island.

There was a good wind and they covered the distance quickly. Kendra tacked back and forth with growing confidence. She still made little mistakes, but she felt she had turned the corner in her struggles with sailing. Although Ryan would have liked to be the one at the tiller, he sensed Kendra's newfound focus and was content to let her steer.

The island grew larger as they approached. There was no sign of any other boats around. Kendra sailed to the place where they had tied up previously and brought *Pegasus* into shore. They secured the boat and, making sure they had spare batteries for the flashlights, quickly made their way to the lighthouse.

Ryan opened the door using the same combination as before. Turning on their flashlights, they made their way through the storage room into the lighthouse, with Meg leading the way. Nobody spoke. They were all on edge, wondering if the secret door would still be as they left it. Or would the mysterious Owen Gates have reached it before them?

Daylight filtered down from the top of the lighthouse, illuminating the spiral steps leading up. Meg immediately went over to the trap door that led to the basement, sniffing at the handle. Claire pushed her gently aside so she could lift up the door. It was heavy and took two of them to lift it, the hinges creaking softly as it rose.

As soon as the door was open, Meg scurried down the steps into the darkness.

"Where's she going?" said Ryan, watching her curiously. "She doesn't think she's going to find another ball down there, does she?"

Whatever the reason, Meg wanted to be the first one into the basement. The others followed more cautiously, shining their flashlights in front of them. They didn't want to slip on the steps or the wet floor. Once they were all down, Kendra shone her light on the knothole in the wall and stuck her finger through it. She felt around until her finger found the curved hook and she pulled upward. Just like before, the latch opened and she was able to swing the wooden panel open, revealing the cave inside.

They hesitated before going further. Even with two flashlights and fresh batteries, the cave seemed dark and foreboding. After a moment or two, Claire stepped forward, ducking through the panel opening and into the cave. There was a splash as she put her foot down and she felt water soaking into her sneaker. The cave floor was covered in water a few inches deep. Claire tried not to think about what might be in the water as she put her other foot forward.

"Can you see anything?" said Ryan, poking his head through the opening behind her.

Claire shone her light around the cave, which wasn't very high. She could only just stand upright. The walls and roof of the cave were of rough grey rock, with irregular bumps and outjutting rocks.

"I don't see anything yet," she replied. She took another step forward, and then another. Behind her she heard a splash as Ryan stepped into the cave. She stopped and shone the light around again. This time she noticed a crack on one side of the cave, forming a shelf at about knee level. She took another few steps and shone her light into the crack. The light reflected off something metal. Pushed to the back of the shelf was a steel box, and the light was reflecting off an old padlock!

"I found something!" she cried. Her voice echoed around the cave, deafening them all. "I found a box!" she said, more quietly this time.

"Let's see," said Ryan, peering over her shoulder. Kendra and Nathan crowded into the cave as well, and even Meg hopped in after them, nosing about between their legs.

It was about the size of a large toolbox and made of black steel, with a handle on top. It was quite rusted along the edges and around the handle. At the front was a steel clasp and through that a large padlock. The padlock was dull and tarnished, but still secure.

"What's in it?" said Kendra. Claire reached in and pulled on the box. It didn't move.

"Ugh, it weighs a ton," she grunted. Ryan pulled from the other side, but even together they were unable to move it.

"We can open it where it is," said Ryan, "if we can unlock it."

"I guess your combination trick won't work this time," Claire said to Ryan ruefully. This lock required a key.

"Do you think the key is somewhere in the lighthouse?" said Kendra.

"I don't remember seeing a key anywhere," said Claire. "But we can take a look." Kendra and Nathan took one of the flashlights and backed out of the cave. They returned a short while later, without having found any keys.

"That's probably not too surprising," said Ryan. "I wouldn't expect the keys to be just lying around."

"How are we going to open it then?" said Nathan.

The four children stared at the box, stumped. Ryan shook the lock. Of course, it didn't open, but he noticed the metal clasp twist a bit. He looked at it more closely under the flashlight.

"That clasp is pretty rusted," he said. "I wonder if we could break it off."

"There's a hammer up in the storage room," said Nathan. "I'll go get it." He ran back up the steps and quickly returned with an old hammer. It was rusted as well but seemed fairly solid nonetheless. Claire shone the light while Nathan brought the hammer down on the clasp. The metal bent a little. Nathan continued to whack away at the clasp with the hammer, while the others covered their ears from the echoes reverberating around the cave. After several minutes Nathan stopped for a rest, his arm tired from swinging the hammer.

"Am I getting anywhere?" he panted. Ryan looked at the clasp again.

"I think so," he said. "I see a crack forming where it's welded to the box. Let me try."

He took the hammer from Nathan, who was happy to give it up, and began to bang away at the clasp. The crack got larger and eventually the clasp split from the box entirely. They gave a cheer as Ryan pried the clasp away with the claw of the hammer and twisted the lock free.

Slowly Ryan lifted the lid of the box, revealing a black cloth. He pulled it away, and they all gasped. Glinting brightly in the beam of the flashlight, the box was filled with gold!

"Wow!" said Nathan. "It really is a treasure!"

The others were speechless. Inside the box were hundreds of small gold nuggets, ranging from the size of a pea to one that was as big as a walnut. They picked up the nuggets and stared at them in amazement. The pieces were rough and unevenly shaped, and surprisingly heavy for their small size.

"Do you think this came from the *Alexandria*?" said Kendra in a hushed tone.

"It must have," said Claire. "When the ship sank, whoever owned this gold would have tried to save it. But then they either lost it or were drowned. And later, Henry Cooper the lighthouse keeper must have found it in the wreckage and brought it here."

At one end of the box were two small bags made of rough, heavy cloth and tied up with string. Ryan opened one of them. Inside, it was filled with small flakes of gold. He showed the others, then carefully tied it back up. He opened the other bag and pulled out a handful of gold coins. They were from the United States, with a woman's head and the word 'Liberty' on one side, and an eagle holding a crest on the other. Each one had 'Twenty Dollars' stamped on it.

"So each of these is worth twenty dollars?" asked Kendra, looking at the coin with amazement.

"I bet they're worth a lot more than that now. These coins are from the late 1800's when gold was worth a lot less. Nowadays each of those coins might be worth more than a thousand dollars!" said Ryan.

"And what about all these nuggets? What are they worth?"

"Enough to justify buying the island," said Claire soberly, reminding them why they had come in the first place.

"And now we can buy the island with it!" said Kendra. "And then we can live in the lighthouse!"

"Wait a minute," said Claire. "This box belongs to whoever owns the island, not to us. And right now that's the government."

"Until midnight," added Ryan. "After that it belongs to the numbered company owned by Jonathan Cooper and Owen Gates."

"So what do we do?" asked Nathan.

Claire thought for a moment. "The box is too heavy to bring back," she said. "Besides, we don't need to bring it all back with us. We can just bring a few samples and tell them how much there is. That should be enough to stop the sale."

"What about Owen Gates?" said Ryan. "If he gets a rental boat and comes out here, he might find the box and steal it."

"We'll put everything back the way it was. I don't think he'll find it. It was a fluke that we found it, only because Meg went searching for that ball."

"All right," said Ryan, reaching to take some nuggets out of the box. "Let's each take a few and get going. There's no time to lose!"

They each took two nuggets and a coin and put them in their pockets. Then they closed the lid of the box. Exiting the cave, they closed the panel and made sure it was secure. One by one they went back up the steps to the main floor of the lighthouse with

Claire and Ryan gently closing the trapdoor behind them. Claire brushed some dirt over it so it looked undisturbed, the way they had found it the day before.

Nathan was just stepping into the storage room from the lighthouse when the door to the outside closed and the room went dark. Meg began to bark.

"The wind must have blown the door shut," Nathan said. Then he heard a scraping noise outside the door, followed by a click. He rushed across the room. Grasping the doorknob, he turned and pushed. The door didn't open. He pushed again, harder this time, but to no avail. Nathan threw himself against the door as hard as he could, but it didn't budge.

He turned to face the others, who were staring at him with shocked faces.

They were locked in!

15

S·O·S

"It's probably just stuck," said Claire. "Let me try." She pushed Nathan aside and, turning the knob with one hand, gave the door a shove with her shoulder. But it didn't open. Not quite able to believe it, they all tried pushing together, but it wouldn't open.

"How could it have shut?" wondered Ryan aloud. "I hooked the padlock on the latch so it couldn't close on us."

As he spoke, they heard the sound of a boat motor starting up. Kendra cocked her head, listening. Then she tore off through the storage room and up the steps of the lighthouse. The others stared at each other a moment and then ran after her.

Kendra took the steps two at a time until she reached the light room. She ran to the window and peered. Motoring away from the island was a small white powerboat with a lone man at the wheel. Kendra yelled out and waved her hands frantically, trying to draw the man's attention. But he continued to drive away.

"I don't think he's going to see you," said Nathan, who had come up the stairs and was now standing behind her. "He's facing the other way."

Kendra nodded glumly, although she continued to wave an arm half-heartedly in the hopes the man would turn around. Claire and Ryan had joined them and were staring out at the disappearing boat.

"I'm not sure he'd stop even if he did see us," she said slowly. Ryan gave her a quizzical look.

"That's one of the rental boats from the marina," she continued. "And I'll bet that the man driving it is the man we saw, Owen Gates."

Kendra's eyes widened. "You mean he followed us here! And then he locked us in!" Claire nodded grimly.

"But why would he lock us in?" asked Ryan. "That makes no sense. If he thinks we know where the treasure is, why wouldn't he just take it from us? Or wait until we left and then sneak in and take it."

"Because…" Claire looked at her watch. "In six hours he's going to own it anyway. All he needs to do is make sure nobody finds out about the treasure until after midnight, at which point he owns the island and everything on it!"

There was a collective groan. "Then we've got to find a way out of here!" said Kendra. "There's got to be another exit!"

They set to work looking for another way out of the lighthouse. First they tried the other door to the lighthouse. Ryan half-heartedly tried opening it, but he already knew it was locked from the outside. They scanned the walls of the lighthouse and the storage room with their flashlights, but there weren't any other doors or windows. Nathan noticed light coming from a corner in the storage room, but when they investigated it was just a small vent opening, far too small for anyone to fit through. Even Meg sniffed around the doors, seeming to realize they needed a way out.

They climbed the stairs back up to the light room and looked around. Kendra looked out one of the broken windows, but it was a sheer drop down the side of the lighthouse to the rocks below.

"What about the secret cave?" said Ryan. "We know it leads out somewhere because Meg's ball came in that way."

"That crack was too small for anyone to go through," said Nathan.

"We may as well try," said Claire. "We don't have any better options."

They went back down into the basement and opened up the secret panel in the wall. As Kendra was the smallest, she took the flashlight and ventured into the cave toward the faint light coming from the end. The cave got narrower and narrower and soon she was on her hands and knees. She kept going even while the rough rock was hurting her knees. Finally she had to crawl on her stomach to get any further. Grazing her head on the roof of the cave, she momentarily panicked. What if I get stuck in here?

Breathing deeply, she paused a moment before continuing. At last she reached the end and, rolling onto her back, looked up. She could see a small sliver of blue sky through the crack in the rock. But there was no way she could go any further. The crack was far too narrow. It had only just been large enough for Meg's ball to fall through. Kendra slowly wriggled her way back through the cave.

"There's no way out through there," she announced once she was able to stand up again. Claire sighed. She had thought that would be the case but had held onto a small hope that Kendra would be able to find a way out.

"Now what do we do?" said Ryan.

"Sit and wait," said Claire in response. "Eventually mom and dad will start looking for us. But they aren't expecting us back until later and I'm afraid by the time they get search and rescue to send a boat out here it will be too late."

"Well let's eat our dinner while we wait," said Nathan. "I'm starving!"

Claire gave him a pained look. "Our dinner is on the boat, I'm afraid."

Nathan's eyes widened. "No food? What will we do? We'll starve to death!"

"You're not going to starve in one day!" said Claire. But she knew what Nathan was like when he needed food. And she was starting to feel a bit hungry herself.

They decided to go back up to the light room to wait. It was the brightest room, so they could save the batteries in their flashlights. And it was the nicest place to wait, with its panoramic views over the strait. They sat down on the floor and played word games to pass the time. Every so often they would look out to see if there were any boats nearby. But there were very few boats out at all, and the ones that could be seen were far in the distance.

The sun dropped low in the sky and eventually sank below the horizon in a fiery ball of red. They watched as the clouds on the horizon lit up in magnificent hues of red and pink. It was a terrific sunset and they had the best spot to watch it from. Finally the colours faded and the sky turned dark. Lights began to twinkle from the houses on the shore.

That gave Kendra an idea. "Maybe we could use our flashlights to signal for help, now that it's dark. Send an S-O-S or something. After all, we are in a lighthouse."

Ryan looked at her skeptically. "Nobody will see these little flashlights," he said. "Look, the lights on shore are only little specks and those are way brighter than our lights."

They lapsed into silence again. But Nathan was thinking about what Kendra had said. For a moment he forgot about how hungry he was and thought of the books about lighthouses he had been reading. There might be a way to send a signal, he thought, if only they could magnify the light.

Suddenly he jumped to his feet. "I've got it!" he exclaimed. "We can send an S-O-S! We just have to use the old Fresnel lens!"

"We can send an S-O-S!"

~16~

Unexpected Help

"The what?" said Claire.

"The Fresnel lens!" said Nathan exasperatedly. "That thing!" He pointed at the big glass lens in the middle of the light room.

"Oh, right. I'd forgotten what it was called."

"How can we use it?" said Ryan. "There's no light in it anymore."

"We can put a flashlight inside it. Then the lens will concentrate the light so it can be seen from a long distance away!"

Claire looked dubious. "Even with the lens to magnify it, isn't that flashlight way too small?"

"Not really," said Nathan. "The lights in old lighthouses weren't that strong. In fact, they used to use oil lamps, which weren't very bright at all. They relied on a Fresnel lens in order for it to be seen."

"I thought the light has to turn inside though?" said Ryan, looking at the mechanism inside the old lens.

"That's just so it shines in all directions," said Nathan. "We can just point it in one direction at a time to send a signal."

"How did you learn all this?" said Kendra, looking at Nathan with admiration.

"I learned it from those books I took out of the library," he answered, looking pleased with himself.

"Ahh. So they weren't just for driving us crazy with lighthouse trivia." Claire laughed. "All right, let's try sending a signal."

She handed her flashlight to Nathan. He stuck it inside the lens through the opening in the bottom. The room lit up with little squares of light. Nathan moved the flashlight around until it was pointing sideways. A beam of light shone out, lighting up dust particles in the air.

"Wow, it really works!" exclaimed Kendra.

"Tilt it down a bit," said Claire. "You're pointing up into the sky." Nathan angled the light down slightly until it was horizontal.

"What message shall we send?" asked Kendra.

"Just an S-O-S," said Ryan. "We don't know any other Morse code, do we?"

Claire shook her head. "And even if we did, nobody seeing it would know what it meant. But everyone knows S-O-S."

Nathan began to turn the flashlight on and off, sending out the signal. Three short flashes for S, followed by three long flashes for O, then another three short flashes for S again. When he finished he turned the light off and the room went dark.

"Keep going," said Claire. "If anyone sees it, they'll need to see it a few times to be sure it's an S-O-S."

Nathan began again. Three short flashes, three long flashes, three short flashes, then off. He waited a few moments and then began again.

"Hopefully anyone who sees it will know it's an S-O-S and not just the lighthouse light flashing," said Ryan as he watched the beam of light go on and off.

"Most people seeing it will know the lighthouse has been inactive for years," said Claire. "So they should wonder why it's flashing and pay attention."

After a while Nathan withdrew his arm from inside the lens and groaned, stretching it out. "My arm is sore," he said. "Somebody else take a turn."

Ryan took over sending out the signal. He shone the light in a different direction. "That way, more people will see it," he said.

One by one they each took turns holding the flashlight inside the lens and flashing out the S-O-S. Short-short-short. Long-long-long. Short-short-short.

On and off it went, sending its signal out into the dark night. When the light started to grow dim, they changed the batteries and began again. Short-short-short. Long-long-long. Short-short-short. Long-long-long—

"Hey, you're doing O-S-O!" said Ryan, as Nathan was starting another round of signals.

Nathan gave him a tired look. "That's because I'm too hungry to think properly," he said. He slumped down beside the lens.

They were all tired and hungry. Although they'd been signalling for more than an hour, so far there had been no response to their S-O-S. Kendra stifled a yawn. She felt her eyelids drooping.

Suddenly, her eyes snapped open again. In the distance she heard a faint whine. She listened for a bit and it seemed to get a little louder.

"What's that?" she said.

The others listened carefully. Then they all jumped to their feet and rushed to the window to look out.

"There it is!" cried Nathan, pointing to a tiny speck of light in the distance. "It's a boat!"

"It's a pretty small boat," said Claire. "It's just got a single white light, no running lights."

Ryan rushed back to the Fresnel lens and began to flash out the S-O-S once again, this time in the direction of the boat. Claire, Kendra, and Nathan continued to peer out the window at the speck of light, which was slowly getting bigger.

When the light had almost reached the island it veered off to the left and then came in to shore next to *Pegasus*. Now they could see the outline of the boat. It was very small, even smaller than *Pegasus*, with two people on board. Ryan stopped signalling and joined them at the window.

"It looks like an inflatable dinghy," he said.

The two figures hopped out of the dinghy and pulled it up on the shore. Then they ran toward the lighthouse. Ryan shone the flashlight down through one of the broken windows.

"Help, we're locked in!" they all cried together. "Let us out!"

The figures stopped running and looked up. "Claire?" one of them called out.

Inside the lighthouse, Claire groaned. "I'm glad someone's come to rescue us," she muttered. "But why did it have to be the Mitchell brothers?"

~17~

Success

Claire was correct. It was indeed Matthew and Flint Mitchell who had seen the S-O-S signal and had come to investigate.

"They probably won't even let us out," said Nathan with a scowl.

"I'm sure they will," said Kendra as she hurried down the stairs. "Come on."

The Mitchells were hammering on the door when they reached the bottom. Ryan called out the combination and they could hear the boys fiddling with the lock on the other side of the door. Suddenly it opened.

"What are you guys doing here?" asked Flint, shining his flashlight in their eyes. "How did you lock yourselves in?"

"We didn't lock ourselves in!" sputtered Claire indignantly. "Someone else locked us in!"

"It was the man who wants to buy the island!" said Ryan.

"Because we found the treasure he's looking for!" added Kendra.

"And now we can stop the sale!" said Nathan. "If we hurry!"

The Mitchells looked at them disbelievingly.

"Oh, never mind. Just take us back to Maple Harbour," said Claire. "I'll explain everything on the way."

She started off toward the Mitchells' boat. Matthew and Flint, after hesitating a moment, ran after her. Together they pushed the dinghy into the water and hopped in. Claire looked over at *Pegasus*, which was still bobbing gently in the waves where they had left it.

"Do you think you can sail back in the dark?" she called out.

"I guess so," answered Ryan, a bit unsure.

"Sure we can," said Kendra. Suddenly she felt quite confident about her sailing. The wind was light and the moon was out so they could see quite clearly. She didn't think it would be any different from sailing in the daytime.

"I'll meet you at the marina," said Claire. "Don't forget the lights. They're in the hatch."

She gave a wave as Matthew started the motor with a roar and the little dinghy sped off toward Maple Harbour.

Ryan, Kendra, Nathan, and Meg watched them go before getting ready to leave themselves. Meg whimpered a little at seeing Claire go off without them. Ryan ran back to lock the lighthouse while Nathan dug around in the hatch for the boat lights. There was a red/green combination light for the bow and a white light for the stern. He and Kendra clipped them into position and turned them on.

When Ryan returned from the lighthouse, Kendra and Nathan were waiting for him in *Pegasus*, with Meg in the bow. Nathan had already pulled out the cooler bag and was digging around in it for something to eat. Ryan hopped in and they pushed off.

It was a new experience for all of them, sailing in the dark. Ryan was a little nervous at first, wondering how they would see to keep the sails filled and the boat on course. But in the light of the moon it was easy to see the white sail rising above them. And the lights on shore showed them where to go. Soon he relaxed.

Kendra thought that sailing in the dark was one of the most amazing things she'd experienced. It was a beautiful night, with the wind warm and stars twinkling in the sky. Nobody spoke and there was only the sound of waves lapping against the bow and the odd creak of the boom or a pulley. The darkness made her feel like she was completely alone in the middle of nowhere, even though she could see the outlines of Ryan and Nathan, and the lights on shore were not too far away.

They were anxious to return home, but the wind was light and it took a long time to get back. Finally the marina came into view, its red and green flashing lights marking the entrance.

"Red right returning," muttered Nathan from the bow where he was perched.

"What's that?" asked Ryan, not understanding.

"Red, right, returning," repeated Nathan. "It means you keep the red lights on your right-hand side when you're coming back into the harbour. That way you won't go on the wrong side of the channel and hit a rock or the shore."

"Oh, that's a good way to remember," said Kendra. She knew that on boats, red was for left and green for right. But when you were coming back in, the left side of the harbour entrance would be on your right. She thought that on a very dark, moonless night it would be easy to miss the entrance and run into the breakwater instead.

Ryan steered them carefully into the marina, keeping the red flashing light to his right. Once they were inside, they dropped the sail and paddled the rest of the way, not wanting to sail up the narrow channel and risk bumping into any other boats. They took turns paddling until they arrived at the dock they had left from that afternoon. It seemed a very long time ago!

As soon as they touched the dock, Meg hopped out with a joyous little bark. Claire and Aunt Jennie were waiting for them. They both had big smiles on their faces.

"We did it!" Claire exclaimed. "We stopped the sale!"

Claire explained how she had called Aunt Jennie as soon as she had got back to the marina. Aunt Jennie, in turn, had called the government agent at home.

"He wasn't happy about being woken up," said Aunt Jennie with a laugh. "But he agreed to come down to the marina and take a look."

"He still didn't believe me though, even when he saw the nuggets and coins," said Claire. "He didn't think they were real, or that we found them on the island. Just when I was starting to get really frustrated, Sophie walked in."

"You mean the new curator from the museum?" said Kendra.

"That's right. She was able to confirm the coins were real, and she was very excited to hear where we found them. After that, the government agent believed me."

"So what happened then?" asked Ryan.

"Once he was convinced, Mom insisted he halt the sale of the island. After all, the treasure is worth a lot more than the sale price, so that's a significant change in the terms of the offer. He finally agreed, putting a thirty-day freeze on the sale."

"What happens after thirty days?" said Ryan.

"I can't say for sure," said Aunt Jennie. "But I don't think the buyers will be interested once they know the gold has been found. Pete Saunders said the price they were offering was too high for the island alone, so he thinks they must have known there was something more valuable there."

"What about the guy who locked us in the lighthouse?" said Nathan. "Did they catch him?"

Claire shook her head. "We called the police and told them what happened. Officer Sandhu came down to the marina and spoke with the boat rental operator. Someone called Owen Gates did rent a boat today and returned it a few hours ago. But so did a lot of other people, so there's no way of proving that he was the one who locked us in."

Their faces fell.

"Cheer up," said Aunt Jennie. "The important thing is that you've stopped the sale of the island. And that you're home safe and there's no harm done."

Nathan looked at her incredulously. "No harm done!" he exploded. "Mom, I could have died of starvation!"

~18~

The Real Meaning

A few days later, it was Ryan and Kendra's last day in Maple Harbour. That evening they would board the ferry and return to their home in the city. Kendra woke early, in spite of going to bed late the night before. She intended to make the most of her last day so she took Meg, who was the only other one awake, down to the beach for a walk. The sun was just rising and the wet sand sparkled in the morning light. Gulls swooped and circled in the air, squawking at each other as they looked for crabs and mussels on the beach. The air was already warm and it promised to be another beautiful day.

After the others awoke, the rest of the day was spent swimming in the ocean and playing on the beach. Kendra and Nathan built an elaborate sand-castle and then desperately tried to prevent it being washed away by the tide. Everyone jumped off the dock and played Marco Polo in the cool water. Then the four of them lay on the sand, reading and dozing.

In the afternoon they took *Pegasus* out for one last sail, with Kendra and Ryan taking turns at steering.

They sailed close to Opera Island, although they didn't land. The FOR SALE sign was still up on the island.

"Shouldn't they have taken that down?" asked Kendra, pointing to the sign.

"They probably haven't had a chance to come out here yet," said Ryan.

"Well, officially the sale isn't over," said Claire. "It's just on hold for thirty days."

None of them knew what would happen after the thirty days was up. Aunt Jennie had been correct about the buyers though. As soon as the sale was put on hold and the reason given, they withdrew their offer to purchase the island.

"Maybe we'll find out more soon," said Kendra. "Aunt Jennie says she's expecting some news."

"Perhaps," shrugged Claire, as she pointed *Pegasus* toward home.

* * *

After an early dinner of barbecued salmon and corn on the cob, followed by fresh-baked apple pie, the four children and Meg squeezed into Aunt Jennie's car.

"Move over Meg," said Nathan. "You're squishing my stomach."

"If you hadn't eaten so many pieces of apple pie, your stomach wouldn't be taking up so much room," said Kendra, laughing.

Aunt Jennie drove them to the ferry terminal, which was crowded with cars as tourists returned home from their holidays. Summer was coming to an end and the sun was already low in the sky by the time the big ship steamed into sight. Ryan and Kendra would be walking on as foot passengers and their parents would pick them up on the other side. They watched the ferry with mixed emotions, anxious to see their parents again but wishing they didn't have to leave Maple Harbour so soon.

The ferry doors swung open and the foot passengers streamed off in advance of the cars. Kendra spotted Officer Sandhu amongst them and she waved. He waved back and came over to chat with them.

"Hi Raj," said Aunt Jennie.

"Hi everyone," he said. "I have some news for you that I think you'll be interested in." He had a mysterious smile on his face. "We've made an arrest!"

"Who?" they all asked at the same time.

"Your friend Owen Gates."

"He's not our friend!" said Nathan indignantly.

"Did you arrest him for locking us in the light-house?" asked Kendra.

"No," he replied. "Unless he admits to it, I don't think we'll ever prove that was him. Instead, we've charged him with bribery."

Bribery! There was a stunned silence as they digested this news.

"How did that come about?" said Ryan after a moment had passed.

"Well, it started when you kids told me about Opera Island being up for sale. It sounded strange to me, so I made a few calls to some colleagues in the federal government. None of them could remember a case where a historic lighthouse was put up for sale. The sale was authorized by somebody fairly new in the department, a woman named Kathy Fischer. She authorized it based on some obscure policy adopted decades ago and long forgotten by most people.

"Later," he continued, "when the gold was discovered and you told me your suspicions about Owen Gates, I did some more digging. It turns out that Owen Gates and Kathy Fischer used to work together. About a month ago, a large sum of money was transferred from the numbered company that was buying the island, to a bank account associated with Ms. Fischer. When she was confronted with that information, she confessed to the whole thing. Shortly after, we were able to lay charges against Owen Gates for bribing an official."

"Wow!" said Claire. "That's big news. What about the other guy named as a company director, Jonathan Cooper? Wasn't he involved?"

"Not in the bribery, apparently," said Officer Sandhu. "He was friends with Mr. Gates and enlisted his help to buy the island and find the treasure. But it was Owen Gates who paid Kathy Fischer to assist them."

"But how did they know the treasure was on the island?" asked Nathan. "I've never understood that."

"Jonathan Cooper was the great-grandson of Henry Cooper, the original lighthouse keeper. His father used to tell him stories about the lighthouse that had been passed down to him, including the one about the treasure. But it was more than just a rumour for him—he had one of the nuggets, which convinced him the story was true. And it was enough to convince Owen Gates as well."

Everyone was quiet as they let this information sink in.

"Well, I've got some more news," said Aunt Jennie. They looked at her expectantly.

"I've known a little bit about what was going on with the investigation, as the government has been keeping the village council informed. And now the government has officially stopped the sale for good!"

Everyone cheered. This was good news indeed.

"And not only that, but they've agreed to turn the island into a protected park, due to the importance of it as a nesting site."

Everyone cheered again. This was even better news!

"Well, I guess that wraps things up," said Officer Sandhu.

"Not quite," said Ryan. "We still don't know why it's called Opera Island!"

Officer Sandhu looked surprised. "I can tell you that."

"Is it because of the singing sea lions?" asked Kendra.

"Or the singing mermaids," said Nathan, remembering the story told to them by Ned McCaffrey.

Officer Sandhu laughed. "I'm afraid it's got nothing to do with sea lions or mermaids. Or anyone else singing for that matter. It's an old acronym going all the way back to World War II. It stands for Ocean Patrol Emergency Region A. It was used to designate search areas in the strait, which included the waters around that island. After a while, the name stuck."

"That's boring," said Kendra.

"I guess that's why Ned just stuck to the story his dad told him about the mermaids," said Nathan.

"Sorry, kids," Officer Sandhu said apologetically. "Anyway, I'd better get going." He said goodbye and walked off toward the parking lot.

"What about all the money that was raised to buy the island?" asked Claire, after Officer Sandhu had left. "What will happen to that?"

"I can't say for sure," said Aunt Jennie. "But it's been suggested that it might be used to make repairs on the lighthouse, or for seabird rehabilitation."

"It would sure be nice to see the old lighthouse restored to its original condition," said Ryan.

"And go back to using that Fresnel lens as the signal," said Nathan. "I could be the new lighthouse keeper!"

"Wouldn't you be lonely out there?" asked Aunt Jennie.

"Nah, it would be great."

"There would be no fresh food. You'd have to eat everything out of cans and boxes," said Claire.

"That's all right," said Nathan. "I like food that comes in boxes."

"No more fresh salads," said Aunt Jennie. Nathan shrugged indifferently.

"No more apple pie," said Kendra.

Nathan gulped. "Maybe it's not such a good idea."

Suddenly, the ship's whistle blew and they saw that all the other foot passengers had finished boarding. A crew member was standing at the end of the ramp, waving at them to hurry up. Ryan and Kendra said a quick goodbye and ran for the ferry, lugging their suitcases behind them. Once they were safely on board they turned back to look. Aunt Jennie, Claire, Nathan, and Meg were all standing at the end of the ramp, waving goodbye.

"I forgot to say goodbye to Meg," said Kendra as she waved back. "Goodbye Meg!" she shouted over the sound of the ferry engines.

"I don't think she can hear you," said Ryan.

But Meg must have heard, because she perked her ears up and then barked loudly, once, twice, three times, as if to say, "Come back soon!"

The End

About the Author

Michael Wilson lives in Gibsons, British Columbia with his family. S·O·S at Night is the third book in his Maple Harbour Adventure series for children. His first book, Adventure on Whalebone Island, was shortlisted for the BC Reader's Choice Children's Book Award and Saskatchewan Young Readers' Choice Awards. When not writing, he likes to sail his Flying Junior in the waters of Howe Sound.

***

Did you enjoy reading *S·O·S at Night?* We'd love to hear from you!

Rainy Bay Press
PO Box 1911
Gibsons, BC
V0N 1V0

www.rainybaypress.ca

Look for more adventures with Claire, Ryan, Kendra, Nathan, and Meg, coming soon!

Don't miss the first Maple Harbour Adventure!

Adventure on Whalebone Island

Ryan and Kendra have come to Maple Harbour on the BC coast to spend their summer holidays with their aunt and uncle. They're expecting a leisurely holiday swimming and playing on the beach with their cousins Claire and Nathan. Claire, however, has other ideas—exploring islands in her sailboat and searching for sunken treasure. But what's hidden on mysterious Whalebone Island? Have the four of them come across a secret that others don't want discovered?

Join Ryan, Kendra, Claire, Nathan, and their dog Meg as they try to solve the mystery of a missing boat. What awaits the children is an even bigger, more dangerous mystery! I couldn't put this book down!   Colleen H., teacher

Shortlisted for the:

BC Reader's Choice Children's Book Award
(Chocolate Lily Award)
&
Saskatchewan Young Readers' Choice Awards
(Diamond Willow Award)

And look for the second Maple Harbour Adventure!

The Mystery of the Missing Mask

Ryan and Kendra have returned to Maple Harbour on the British Columbia coast to visit their cousins Claire and Nathan. But the sleepy little town has been rocked by the news that a valuable Indigenous mask has been stolen, only days after it arrived at the local museum! While museum officials and the police search for answers, the four children and their new friend Tyler stumble upon a series of exciting clues. As they enjoy their summer holidays, not everything is what it seems. Join the four friends on another unforgettable summer of adventure!

Kids won't be able to put down the second book in the Maple Harbour Adventure series. The suspense will keep them on the edge of their seats! Gabriele K., teacher

Young readers will be thoroughly entertained by this story of children outwitting adults to solve the crime. Jane A., librarian

Highly recommended. Alicia Cheng, CM Magazine

If you're looking for great adventures for kids, then this is the book for you. Fergus, age 8